"Fire!"

Livy came awake slowly. Her weary mind tumbled over her thoughts. Hayden had spoken but his word didn't make sense. The fire shouldn't have come this close so soon. He had to be waking them for the trek to the helicopter's landing spot.

"Wake up, everybody! We need to get moving."

She rose slowly, blinking her eyes. Behind the ridge, back the way they had come, flames lit the sky. That jolted her senses into alertness. She leaped to her feet and looked around. Hayden stooped to grab his backpack and slide the straps over his shoulders.

Chris ran back from the bend on the trail, straight toward Hayden. "It's a fire all right...and it's close. We have to get out of here."

Livy shook her head. "The fire was almost out when I went to sleep."

Hayden met her gaze, his dark eyes once more lit by the flames of the campfire. "It's a new one. I spotted it and asked Chris to check it out."

Livy's lips parted in surprise as his words registered. A new fire. Started by someone following them. Someone behind them, setting fires and driving them toward the complex fire like rats in a lab maze.

Tanya Stowe is a Christian fiction author with an unexpected edge. She is married to the love of her life, her high school sweetheart. They have four children and twenty-one grandchildren, a true adventure. She fills her books with the unusual—mysteries and exotic travel, even a murder or two. No matter where Tanya takes you—on a trip to foreign lands or a suspenseful journey packed with danger—be prepared for the extraordinary.

Books by Tanya Stowe

Love Inspired Suspense

Mojave Rescue
Fatal Memories
Killer Harvest
Vanished in the Mountains
Escape Route
Yosemite Firestorm

Visit the Author Profile page at LoveInspired.com.

YOSEMITE
FIRESTORM

TANYA STOWE

LOVE INSPIRED SUSPENSE
INSPIRATIONAL ROMANCE

LOVE INSPIRED® SUSPENSE
INSPIRATIONAL ROMANCE

Recycling programs for this product may not exist in your area.

ISBN-13: 978-1-335-58765-7

Yosemite Firestorm

Love Inspired
22 Adelaide St. West, 41st Floor
Toronto, Ontario M5H 4E3, Canada
www.LoveInspired.com

Printed in U.S.A.

Yea, though I walk through the valley of the
shadow of death, I will fear no evil: for thou art with me;
thy rod and thy staff they comfort me.
—*Psalm* 23:4

This book is dedicated to the park rangers,
past and present, who work so hard to keep Yosemite
beautiful and safe for the rest of us.

ONE

Olivia Chatham pulled her ranger Jeep into the parking lot of the hiking trail near Yosemite's Tuolumne Meadows and groaned. Another vehicle was parked in the lot's corner. It was late in the day. She'd hoped that when she finally finished her workday, all the visitors would be gone from this slightly remote trail.

Apparently that's not going to happen.

Shaking her head, Livy grabbed her baseball cap, backpack and a bottle of water and opened the Jeep door. One visitor would not spoil her hike. She wouldn't let them. Not when she'd been waiting all day for the chance to unwind.

This was just her second day in the meadows, but every day had been loaded with stress as she transitioned to a new location—filling in for her best friend, Jenna Holguin, who was on maternity leave.

Jenna's and Livy's fathers were good friends. The two girls grew up climbing together. When Livy's mother began her downward spiral, climbing was Livy's escape and Jenna stood beside her through it all. There was nothing Livy wouldn't do for Jenna, so when she heard that the ranger set to take Jenna's place during maternity leave had the flu, Livy jumped in and volunteered to spend the week up here until the other ranger was back on her feet. The last few weeks of Jenna's pregnancy had been rough, and Livy was glad to take this worry off her friend's mind so Jenna could concentrate on the baby that was due any minute.

That said, though, Livy couldn't wait to get back to her duties in Yosemite Valley, fifty miles away. Not that her duties there were any easier. The crowds were larger and her duties more complicated. It was just that every year during October, climbers from around the world flocked to Yosemite for events.

The park's nine granite peaks, like El Capitan and Half Dome, distinguished it from other national parks. They crisscrossed the park making Yosemite the destination choice of many climbers all year long. But Yosemite Valley with its amazing views, steep cliffs and accessibility was the perfect place for this major October event…and the perfect home base for Livy. Climbing month started in a little over a week and she couldn't wait to get back and jump in to the festivities.

Livy took a deep breath and cast her eye over the distance. Black clouds of smoke darkened the horizon—far away for now, but fires could spread quickly. According to the latest reports, this one shouldn't be an issue for them…but Livy and the other rangers at Toulumne Meadows were on alert, just in case they needed to evacuate the visitors in the campgrounds.

But for right now, the air was clear, and Livy was headed for the trail. She fitted her cap better on her head and hitched the backpack over one shoulder.

As she passed, her gaze automatically glanced over the license plate of the other vehicle. She paused when she recognized the rented car. The driver, Mr. Miller, had been involved in an altercation with a store employee a few days before Livy left the valley. She had been the ranger on duty and was called to mediate the situation. She broke up the argument between Mr. Miller and the store employee. Her report about the disagreement resulted in the store's firing of the contract employee. She felt bad, but it wasn't the first run-in she'd had with Dennis Ludlow. They had history.

She closed her eyes just thinking about Dennis and their uncomfortable scenes. He wasn't a bad-looking man, with a heart-shaped faced, a strong jaw and straight nose. He always appeared neat and clean with his brown hair swept to the side. But there was something about him, something sneaky. She couldn't put her finger on it but she always felt he was thinking something he was not saying. He was an intense, unpopular employee with the other workers and rangers. He'd had trouble fitting in. Livy had felt sorry for him and tried to befriend him. Dennis mistook her friendship for something more and began trailing her around the park, showing up at all her work events. She even caught him parked outside her small cabin at the ranger headquarters.

She'd confronted the issue head-on by talking to Dennis and putting an end to their friendship. But of course, Dennis took it badly and avoided her. The fact that her report about the confrontation with Mr. Miller resulted in his termination only added salt to Dennis's wounded ego. As he loaded his possessions into his car, she made an effort to ease the trouble between them with some kind words. But he didn't appreciate her efforts and drove away from the park with one last sullen, angry glance.

Livy sighed. As a ranger, she constantly dealt with visitors who were having bad days. Add to that the challenges of managing almost 750,000 acres of national parkland, wild animals and natural disasters, and confrontations like the one she had with Dennis didn't make her job any easier. But the benefits were the spectacular views from mountaintops and cliffs that challenged her.

Today she was going to focus on the view at the top of this trail and not the past. She took one last look at the car before heading toward the trailhead.

The sun was bright and warm, even here at this higher elevation. Livy hadn't gone far before she felt the heat, and she let herself enjoy it while it lasted. In another hour or so, the sun would dip behind the distant peaks and the air would grow cold quickly. Drastic changes—in temperature or other weather conditions—were part of the life here at Yosemite. She never left home without her backpack full of all-weather accommodations.

Moving quickly, she hurried up the trail. After a long while, she smelled something.

Smoke.

Not the distant traces of fire she'd seen off on the horizon but something burning *close by*. Had a new blaze started?

Always in tune with the threat of fire, she spun around, searching the skies. Sure enough, smoke now filled the sky behind her near the parking lot. Running, she made her way up to a switchback where she could look down the mountain to the base of the trail. Fire had consumed the brush along one corner of the parking lot and was even now licking the side of Mr. Miller's car. How had it grown so large, so fast?

The answer to that didn't matter. What *was* important was the fact that it was climbing the trail. The way down the mountain was completely blocked. One large pine tree burst into flames and exploded, shooting fire and debris into the sky like a rocket. The booming sound made Livy flinch and step back. Flames raced up both sides of the clearly marked trail, licking the edges like a hungry monster.

How was she going to get off the mountain? Panic swept over her for one long moment, and she gasped for breath. Catching herself, she recited her favorite Bible verse out loud.

"Yea, though I walk through the valley of the shadow of death, I will fear no evil: for thou art with me."

Her breathing eased. Her mind stopped racing. She took several deep gulps of air and calm flowed through her. She had to report this. Because the danger of fire was so intense, she always carried her radio, even when she was off the clock. She clicked on and reached the main switchboard.

"This is Ranger Chatham in Tuolumne Meadows reporting a fire."

When the operator finally responded, Livy gave her the coordinates and as many details as she could.

"This trail ends on a steep cliff. There's no easy way down for us except for the way we came up, but now it's blocked."

"We? Is there someone else on the trail?"

"I believe there's at least one other person. There's a second car besides mine in the parking lot. A small SUV. I think it belongs to a visitor named Miller. I've spoken to him a couple of times. He's travelling alone. He's an experienced hiker but doesn't climb. I can make my way down the cliff at the top of the trail, but I don't think he can. I'm sure he's aware of the fire. No one on this trail could miss it. But he hasn't returned. You'd better send the search and rescue squad and emergency services, too. I'm going to attempt to find Mr. Miller and bring him across the ravine access we use to repair the trail…unless he's already started climbing down the backside."

Livy's heart skipped a little beat as she said the words. She didn't want to think about an inexperienced climber going down that cliff.

"If we're not on the Tioga Pass Road when search and rescue arrive, we'll be on the cliff at the top of the trail."

"Roger that," the operator responded. "Take care, Ranger Chatham."

Livy clicked off, tucked the radio back into her pack, zipped it closed and started to run. Moving at a brisk pace, she quickly came to the path that crossed over the ravine to the road on the opposite side. Miller wasn't in sight. Gritting her teeth, Livy hurried up the trail again.

They were sending search and rescue. That meant Hayden Bryant would be informed. She felt safer knowing he would be alerted. Maybe it was silly to have such confidence in one man, especially since he hardly even knew she existed. Still, the assurance that Hayden would be informed gave her the courage she needed to move forward.

Smoke was climbing up the mountain making breathing hard and obscuring the path. If she didn't find Mr. Miller soon, they wouldn't have time to get back to the ravine before the fire made crossing it impossible. But as she ran higher, and Mr. Miller didn't appear, she felt a sense of certainty he'd already started to climb down the cliff. That thought put an extra spurt of energy in her run.

If she could just reach him in time, she could guide him down and they might both make it back safely. She rounded the last bend of the trail and saw the lookout with its low fencing to keep hikers from accessing the cliff. The lookout gave a view of the valleys and hills beyond as well as the Tioga Pass Road snaking along the side of the mountain opposite the ravine. The view was the reason Livy loved this hike so much. But today she didn't even pause to enjoy it. Stepping over the border fencing, she hurried to the edge and looked down.

Her worst fear was confirmed. Mr. Miller lay splayed out on a granite shelf, and he wasn't moving. Livy closed her eyes and clamped down on the rising panic. Now was not the time to lose it.

Think, Livy, think!

If he was already dead, she'd just be putting herself in greater danger if she were to climb down to check on him. The safer choice would be to go back to the ravine crossing, wait for Hayden's team, then guide them back here. But what if he was alive and needed immediate assistance?

"Mr. Miller!" She yelled his name, but he didn't respond. She yelled it again, louder. Smoke swirled around her and made her cough, but her loud tone did the job. Mr. Miller must have heard her, because he moved one hand in a feeble attempt to reach up.

He was still alive! There was nothing more for it. She'd have to climb down to assist him. She scanned the cliff. He lay about one hundred feet down. He must have slipped soon after starting the downward climb. The granite boulders were full of cracks and looked easy to navigate but Livy knew better. All those cracks and ledges were loose. Any kind of pressure and weight could make them break loose and she'd find herself beside Miller. Also, granite was slick and grainy, increasing the risk of falling when free climbing. But there was nothing else she could do. She had to get down to him. But no way would she try to climb down in her heavy hiking boots.

Dropping to the ground, she unlaced her boots, sliding them and her socks off. Then she tucked her socks inside, tied the shoes together by the laces and looped them over her neck. Once she reached the ground, she'd need them to cross to the road…if she made it to the ground.

Taking a deep breath, she said a prayer. Then she scoped out the path she would take, finding cracks, finger and toeholds. It used up precious time, but every smart climber knew to plan their route before starting so they didn't find themselves hanging from a rock with no place to go.

Livy found what she thought was a safe way down to Miller and began her descent. Lying on her belly she eased herself over the edge until her toes touched a ledge. She hooked her fingers into a crack and lowered one foot until she found the next ledge. She put her fingers into another crack and slid down to the next ledge, continuing to move down the cliff one tiny crevice and ledge at a time. It was slow going and minutes ticked by. Jagged rock edges scraped her hands and feet. Without chalk her sweaty palms slipped and she had to grip harder to support her weight.

Smoke began to swirl above her. The fire was moving closer. She resisted the natural urge to hurry. One wrong move would see her plunging to her death. That thought made her pause and lean her cheek against the grainy rock in front of her face.

Though I walk through the valley of death, I shall fear no evil.

A wave of peace surged through her. Livy regained the strength to keep moving and soon found herself on the narrow ledge next to Mr. Miller. There was blood on the rock behind his head, and he was bleeding from the ears and his nose—clear indicators that he had a traumatic head injury.

Carefully wedging her back against the rocky cliff, she knelt beside him and clasped his hand. It was cool. His body temperature was dropping. His injuries weren't just serious—they were lethal. The man was dying.

"Mr. Miller, can you hear me?" Sorrow echoed in her tone. She hoped he could hear it. She clasped his hand in both of hers and squeezed.

His eyes fluttered open. It took him a minute to focus but when he did, his lips parted. He tried to speak but only syllables came out, nothing she could recognize as a word.

"Ch...ch..." His efforts faded and his eyes closed.

Livy caught her breath. She was in too precarious a position to attempt CPR. She was afraid to even move. All she could do was hold his hand and hope it comforted him. Tears flowed down her cheeks as she watched his life ebb away.

Suddenly, light flashed in her eyes, a quick reflection of something. She glanced up. Across the way, a car was parked on the pull-out along the highway. A man stood outside the vehicle, and it looked as if he was watching them with binoculars that hung from a cord around his neck. Suddenly, he let them drop, then he spun and ran back to the car.

There was no phone reception at that point on the road. He was probably hurrying away to find help. He couldn't possibly know help was already on the way. But at least when they arrived, he could help the rescue workers pinpoint their location on the cliff.

She sat for a long while with her eyes closed and her back against the rocks. Then smoke began to drift down the side of the cliff.

The fire was getting dangerously close. She was going to have to climb all the way down. She felt weak and drained and dreaded the climb, but there was no other option. Not if she wanted to survive. She sat a moment longer, trying to gather her strength, when the sounds of sirens reached her. The search and rescue trucks pulled to a stop on the road across from the ravine. She saw Hayden climb out of the truck and grab his ropes out of the back. He started down the steep incline with great sideways leaps that plowed up the soil as he lunged down. He was hurrying to reach her.

Livy sobbed in relief, closed her eyes, and waited for him to reach the bottom and then climb up to her position. It took a long time to climb the cliff because he was setting two sets of hooks as he ascended, one for him and one for her. Men waited at the base of the cliff, ready to belay her down. Her adrenaline drained away, and her legs and arms drooped like wet noodles. She would need all their help to climb down.

When Hayden finally reached a point above her, he didn't look at her or say a word until he pounded two hooks in the cliff above them. He clipped the carabiner holding his rope, then hooked another rope for Livy's security. When he finally turned to her and she met his dark-eyed gaze, hot tears coursed down her cheeks again.

"Are you hurt?"

She shook her head. "Mr. Miller is dead, Hayden. He died holding my hand."

"I see that, Livy. I'll take care of him now. You can rest easy."

She nodded again and wiped the tears from her cheeks.

"This is what we're going to do," Hayden announced. "I'm going to swing over to you and balance you for security. Then you're going to stand and slip your legs through a safety harness. Do you think you can do that?"

She nodded.

"All right. Here we go." Pushing his feet against the cliff wall, he leaned back. He literally walked along the wall to Livy and placed his legs on each side of her. Suspended by his ropes above Miller's body, he reached for her.

"All right, put your arms around my neck."

Livy grasped his arms and rose on shaky legs.

He handed her the harness, already connected by a carabiner to the rope hooked into the cliff above them.

Livy was still shaky, but Hayden's arms around her felt like a safe haven. When she had the harness pulled up around her waist and latched into place, she leaned into Hayden and grasped him close, burying her face in his neck. He didn't smell like fires or smoke. He smelled like fresh air and safety. He smelled like home.

After a long while, he quietly murmured, "Come on, Livy. Let's get you down."

She nodded silently.

He took the shoes from around her neck and dropped them on the ledge. "We don't need these tangling up your ropes. Be careful as you go down. Your feet are bleeding."

"They don't hurt."

"They will later, when the numbness goes away. For now, just be careful."

She nodded again. Hayden yelled to the crew below. "She's coming down."

Livy reluctantly released Hayden and began her descent.

Hayden leaned against the wooden support of the lattice covering of the park museum's patio. He ducked back into the shadows, out of sight of the small group gathering for the ceremony. He didn't normally attend the opening ceremonies of climbers month. But he'd decided to make an exception this time. It had only been a week since the fire in Tuolumne Meadows, and park management had pulled a lot of strings to get Livy a commendation in that short amount of time. They'd wanted to give her the award at this bigger-than-usual ceremony and Hayden felt he needed to be here. Livy deserved the recognition and…he cared about her.

She'd attended one of his intermediate climbing classes last winter. As the lead of the Yosemite Search and Rescue team, he held classes throughout the year for rangers and interested residents. He met lots of people, but Livy stood out. Tall and willowy, with white-blond hair, high cheekbones and blue eyes, she looked like the glamorous, camera-ready version of a park ranger that would go on a magazine cover or a movie poster— almost too lovely to be real. Hayden shook his head.

Yeah, you noticed.

Sure, he was attracted to the young ranger. But his interest stopped there. He wouldn't allow the relationship to go any further—even though he got the definite vibe Livy would like it to, especially after the death-lock hug he received the day of the fire. It didn't feel like a "thank you for saving me" kind of embrace. It felt like…more.

Or at least, it had the potential to become more, if he'd let it. Which he wouldn't.

He wasn't interested in a relationship with Livy— with anyone. But especially with her. Livy's cheery, always positive attitude bordered on over-the-top. That kind of purposeful positivity turned him off because he knew for a fact life didn't always turn out for the best. If it did, his best friend would still be alive, and Hayden would still have his career.

He pushed those thoughts away. Today was about

Livy. The park administration was honoring her with a citation for risking her own life in the attempt to rescue Mr. Miller. The press was in attendance as were many climbing celebrities and officials. It was exactly the kind of trumped-up PR activity he usually avoided, especially when his former rival and ex-fiancée were in the park.

Boyd Goldberg attended the event every year. He was a world-renowned climber who focused heavily on his own PR. He had all the big sponsorships…sponsorships that once belonged to Hayden. Three years ago, Hayden had been the up-and-coming climber, setting world records right and left. He had seemed poised to dominate the field—to be *the* climber of his generation. But an accident caused Hayden's best friend and climbing partner, Tommy Kittersal, to fall to his death. To this day, Hayden didn't understand how the clamp he'd inspected himself had broken and sent Tommy plunging hundreds of feet to the rocks below.

Of course, many large companies didn't want their brand associated with a highly publicized accident, so his sponsorships began to disappear. For all intents and purposes Hayden's career was over. But the worst part was the impact it had on his climbing.

Hayden closed his eyes. After all these years, thinking about the accident caused his pulse to race and trembling to overtake his body every time. He still couldn't free-climb. Moving up a cliff without safety ropes used to be as easy to him as breathing. Now free climbing caused him to have a massive panic attack. The last time he had tried, forty feet off the ground he had begun shaking so badly he had to descend. Thankfully, he could still climb anything using a safety harness and ropes. That fact had allowed him to transition into a new career…and it saved him from sinking into a well of depression so deep and dark, he might never have climbed out.

He had successfully joined Yosemite's search and rescue. Now he was the team leader. Saving lives helped him cope with his guilt over not being able to save Tommy. His fear of free climbing remained his best-kept secret, so a low-profile life suited him just fine.

Still, it stung a little every year when Boyd showed up in October, flaunting his celebrity status…and the diamonds on Paulette's fingers. This year was no exception. Only this year, the buzz around Boyd's arrival was louder than usual because instead of just showing up, Boyd was once again attempting to free-climb El Capitan to beat Hayden's record-setting time. Boyd had tried it twice before and failed but bragged to everyone that this was the year he would succeed.

Hayden got the sense that Boyd *needed* to succeed, now more than ever. He had heard rumors that Boyd's career was faltering, that some of his sponsors were threatening to drop him. He also heard that Boyd had been chosen to represent a prestigious climbing school at a resort near Hetch Hetchy, a somewhat secluded area southwest of Yosemite's main valley. Hayden didn't know if the rumors were true but trying to beat Hayden's free climbing record was a useless effort. Boyd's time would be better spent moving forward rather than trying to climb a difficult cliff faster than a record that was created when they were both in their prime.

Hayden didn't miss his former life…well, maybe

he missed free climbing. There were nights when he'd dream about scaling a cliff without a safety harness. The sense of freedom was amazing, but the dream would always end up with him slipping off and falling forever and ever. He'd wake up shaking and sweating. But he never quite forgot the wonderful exhilaration that came in those first few moments of the dream. A feeling he used to have all the time.

But that was all he missed. He'd channeled his competitive spirit into defeating impossible situations in search and rescue scenarios. Bringing someone with injuries out of a dangerous fall could be as satisfying as any record-setting climb. Calming their fear and getting them to safety was all the challenge he needed, and it was the most rewarding feeling he'd ever known. More than the death-defying stunts he used to do to thrill his fans.

Not to mention, he deeply valued the people that search and rescue had brought into his life. That's why he was here today, even though it came with the chance that he might bump into Boyd or Paulette. He was here for Livy, a genuine hero, one who risked her life to help others every day. She deserved the recognition, and he wanted to show his support. So, he would attend the brief ceremony and applaud her effort, then slink into the background again.

The head ranger, Dale Armstead, stepped up to the small podium with the microphone. Dale was in his early fifties, a stocky man with an old-fashioned buzz cut and white threading through his brown hair. Dale was the best supervisor Hayden had ever worked for and he was a fine ranger as well. Standing at the podium in his uniform and the classic ranger flat hat, he looked the part.

Beside him was the mayor of Fresno and another California politician whose name Hayden couldn't remember. Hayden had been introduced to him yesterday, but the man hadn't made an impression. Livy stood beside Armstead. She looked pale, nervous and as uncomfortable as Hayden would have been if he were up there in her place.

Dale flipped on the mic. "How is everyone on this first day of our annual month of climbing events?"

The small crowd clapped and cheered. Armstead nodded and waited for the applause to die down. "It's my pleasure to start this celebration off by honoring one of our own."

The ranger went on, but someone walked up behind Hayden, distracting him from the speaker. He smelled a cloying perfume, one he used to love. He didn't have to turn around to know who it was.

"Hello, Hayden."

That sultry voice—it was her trademark, and one in which she took a great deal of pride. Paulette had been an rising starlet in the French film industry and an avid climber when Hayden first met her. They had a whirlwind romance and fell in love. At least he thought it was love. Apparently, the only thing Paulette loved was his celebrity status.

He turned. The woman he had once wanted to marry looked different. Her cashmere sweater curled up around her chin and swept down her arms, even though it was a warm day. Her stylish fur-lined boots came to her knees. She was the epitome of chic style. But she'd lost weight and even her heavy makeup couldn't hide the dark circles beneath her eyes.

"Hello, Paulette."

"I hoped I'd see you this trip."

Hayden shrugged. "Did you? I can't imagine why."

She released a little sigh. "Please don't make this more difficult than it is, Hayden."

Pausing, he studied her. "Make *what* more difficult? There's nothing between us anymore. Anything we had to say to each other was said three years ago."

She closed her eyes for a long moment. When she opened them, they were shiny with tears. It bothered him that he couldn't tell whether or not they were sincere. Paulette was a trained actress, after all, and she wasn't above using a little manipulation when she wanted to get under his skin. But the thinness, the shadows under her eyes…those hinted that there might be a deeper problem at hand. Maybe something that truly would draw tears from her.

"Yes, and that's what I want to apologize for. I'm sorry about how things ended, Hayden. You were so devastated by Tommy's…" She couldn't seem to bring herself to say the word *death*.

She licked her lips. "Tommy was wonderful, funny and kind. He was my friend, too. When he was gone, I felt lost, Hayden, and I couldn't seem to reach you. You were closed in on yourself. I was sad, lonely, scared— and Boyd was there. Just there when I needed someone."

Hayden's jaw tightened. "Yeah, that seems to be something he does well."

Paulette ducked her head. "Yes, he has that…ability.

But I let him sweep me off my feet. I let him…" She paused again and gave a little shake of her head.

"I let it happen. That was my mistake and I want you to know it's one of the biggest regrets of my life."

Sincerity rang in every syllable. Hayden could hear and see it in her troubled features. She looked away as if gathering strength to say more. After a long pause, she simply shrugged.

"I'm sorry."

He had the feeling there was more she wanted to say, but she'd backed off. He wished she'd said whatever it was she was holding back, wished she'd release the unspoken words from her heart and clear the air between them for good. Not because he wanted to fix things between them but because he wanted closure to finally let the relationship go. The past was gone, as dead as Tommy. Whatever he felt for her was dead, too. But saying that would be churlish after her heartfelt apology.

He inhaled deeply. "I know that took a lot of effort, Paulette. I appreciate it. But it's time to move on. Let the past rest." He turned his body away, back to the podium and the ceremony, which seemed to be concluding.

She stepped up bedside him. "Do you know her, the girl on the podium?"

Hayden's jaw tensed. He'd thought he'd made it clear that they had nothing more to discuss. Not that he didn't appreciate Paulette's confession. It was more that he wanted nothing to do with her husband. He didn't trust Boyd Goldberg as far as he could pick him up and throw him.

"She's a friend," he said without taking his eyes off the group at the podium.

"Good. She's going to need a friend."

There it was. The zinger Hayden had been half expecting. He *knew* there was an ulterior motive behind this little scene.

Folding his arms, he turned back to face Paulette. His face must have telegraphed his anger because she quailed, stepping back slightly.

"What's that supposed to mean?"

She held up a hand defensively. "I'm sorry, Hayden. Truly. I meant it sincerely. She's really going to need a friend. I heard Boyd talking to that politician on the right. The fire she was in, the one that's the reason behind her commendation? The politician mentioned that they found gasoline. Someone started the fire on purpose."

"Wait…what are you saying?"

"The investigator said the fire was started after Olivia parked. Whoever set the blaze saw her car and knew that she was on the trail."

Hayden shook his head. "They think someone purposely set that fire, trapping Livy and Mr. Miller on the mountain?"

Paulette nodded. "That's what the man said."

Hayden took a moment to let that absorb. "If they think an arsonist is operating in the valley, we have a serious problem. We should be mobilizing the rangers and scaling back on our climbing events, not awarding Livy's commendation now. That could have been postponed until a later date."

"The head ranger wanted to cancel it, but the politician came all the way from Sacramento and insisted they go through with it."

Hayden glanced back at the podium. That sounded like Dale Armstead. He was a good, no-nonsense ranger. If he thought his people might be in danger, he would only have gone through with this event under direct pressure.

What didn't make sense was the fact that Boyd knew all about it. What connection did the politician have to Boyd and why would he allow Paulette to hear what seemed to be a private conversation? There could only be one answer.

"Did Boyd send you here to make sure I knew this? Was your apology just an excuse to talk to me?"

Her lips parted in shock, and she took another small step back. "No...of course not. If Boyd knew I was here talking to you, he'd..."

Suddenly, she looked startled. "I have to go. Forget I said anything." Spinning, she hurried through the back entrance and disappeared.

A little surprised, Hayden stared at the empty exit. The encounter had been truly bizarre. He believed Paulette meant what she'd said. She seemed truly concerned about Boyd finding out she talked to him. But Hayden wouldn't put it past Boyd to have planned it, without cluing his wife in. He could easily believe that Boyd let that piece of information about Livy "slip out" in front of Paulette so she would run to tell Hayden when she saw him...and somehow, Boyd knew Paulette wanted to talk to him, would in fact seek out Hayden. Boyd always seemed to instinctively know what others needed or were thinking. It would be just like him to make those moves to trap Paulette. Boyd was at his best when using a manipulative maneuver. That's probably why Paulette ran away so quickly. She'd realized she'd been set up.

But the question that bothered Hayden was why. Why would Boyd go to all that trouble? And what did he have to do with Livy, Mr. Miller and the unknown arsonist?

Now that Hayden knew Boyd was somehow involved, he would have to make sure he found the answers to all his questions.

TWO

Livy stared at her boss, Ranger Armstead, sitting at his desk across from her. She felt numb from head to toe. For one long moment, she couldn't even speak.

Yesterday she was honored as a hero. Today she was facing accusations.

Her lips parted, but nothing came out. She was dumbstruck. Ranger Armstead ducked his head, obviously uncomfortable. He shot a sideways glare at the man standing beside his desk, a fire investigator from the state of California, not the federal parks department. Livy was so surprised she was being questioned, she hadn't even caught his name.

Now the investigator stepped forward and held a small plastic bag in front of her. "Do you recognize this?"

Inside the bag was a slender stick. "It looks like a half-burned sparkler—like the ones I used to play with on the Fourth of July. Is that what was used to start the fire?"

The man nodded. "Several of these were planted all around the meadow and gas was poured over the grass surrounding them. I'm surprised you didn't smell the gas. There was quite a lot of it."

She paused for a moment, remembering the scene as she pulled into the parking lot. Finally, she shook her head. "I don't remember smelling or seeing anything out of the ordinary in the meadow. The only thing I really remember was being a little annoyed that Mr. Miller was on the trail."

"Annoyed? You didn't want him on the trail?"

She made a small sound, almost like a laugh. "A park ranger deals with people's problems all day long. At the end of the day, all I wanted was to take a quiet hike on an empty trail where no one would bother me. I would have been annoyed with anyone there."

"But it is true that you'd had a number of interactions with Mr. Miller in the past?" the man pressed, checking something in the file he was carrying. "There's an official record of an altercation the deceased had with park employee Dennis Ludlow, but you met with Mr. Miller again after that, correct?"

Livy fingered the charms on the bracelet her mother had given her. Each one represented an important event in her life. A small rock for her first successful junior climbing event. A rose for her sixteenth birthday, a cap and scroll for her high school graduation.

Just thinking about the bracelet and the charms on it triggered a wash of emotions through her. Anger. Pride. Sorrow. Fear. Her mother had just been released from a hospital when she gave Livy the bracelet. Her mother told her how proud she was that Livy had overcome their troubled past to become a successful college student and athlete. She'd said how pleased she was that Livy had given her life to Christ and successfully navigated away from the mental health issues that had destroyed her own life. Mom had said, *always follow the path Jesus created for you.* To remind Livy, Mom gave her the miniature initials WWJD, What Would Jesus Do, as a charm.

A month later, her mother was dead by her own hand. Years of struggling with her uncontrolled manic-depressive episodes had driven her mother to that final act of desperation. Her death sent Livy spiraling into the mental health issues she'd avoided, the very issues Mom had praised her for conquering.

Over time, Livy had found her way back. Lots of counseling, her faith, her father's love and Jenna's friendship had helped conquer those mental health issues. Now the bracelet represented all those things, plus her own determination and strength. All the charms were precious to her. Even the one Mr. Miller gave her. It represented another milestone in her life, a lesson learned…even if it was a mistake.

The investigator asked again, his tone indicating irritation at her lack of response. "Did Mr. Miller meet with you again?"

"Yes." Finally able to speak, her voice sounded raspy. "I lost my bracelet the day of the altercation. At the time I didn't know where it had come off, so I searched everywhere. Apparently, Mr. Miller found it and had purchased a small charm of El Capitan for it. He said it was to thank me for my help."

"A gold charm sounds like an expensive gift for just doing your job."

"I thought so, too. I told him that." She frowned, remembering the man's sincere tone. "He told me I had no idea how much my intervention had helped him. He said I might even have saved his life."

"Saved his life? From a disgruntled concession worker?"

She shook her head. "That's what he said. He might have been exaggerating...but it didn't sound that way. I thought it was strange. That whole episode from beginning to end was weird. Dennis and Mr. Miller were arguing about a broken snow globe when I walked into the store. The next thing I knew, Dennis moved toward Mr. Miller like he was going to push him. I put my arm out to stop Dennis. That must have been when my bracelet fell off. It's all in my report...except the part about the charm Mr. Miller gave me. I didn't think that was important."

"It wasn't until you found Miller dead at the base of a cliff."

Shock zapped through Livy, and she studied the investigator. "What do you mean? You sound as if you're accusing me of something."

"I'm simply saying that a stranger gave you an expensive charm for doing your duty and not four days later, he's dead. Don't you think that's unusual?"

For one long moment she was speechless. Heat flushed through her body and bubbled around her lips with a tingling sensation, making it hard to speak.

Anger finally helped her find the words. "What exactly are you getting at? Is that why you showed me that sparkler thing? Are you implying I had something to do with starting that fire?"

"No, of course not, Livy." Ranger Armstead turned his calm gaze on her. "No one's accusing you of anything. He just wants to get the full picture of the situation. Did Miller say anything else? Anything about his connection to Dennis?"

It was hard to take her gaze off the investigator. He made her feel like a snake was hiding in the grass, waiting to strike. She had to force her attention back onto her supervisor. She closed her eyes for one long minute, picturing the scene in her mind. "When I came up to them, Dennis was saying something about watching Mr. Miller. Then he accused him of breaking the snow globe."

She paused. "I didn't think of it before. I just assumed Dennis meant he'd been watching Mr. Miller while he was in the store. But now…do you think Dennis had been watching Mr. Miller *before* that scene in the store? It would explain why the argument got so heated so fast."

The investigator, who had pushed hard at the beginning of the conversation, was now silent. Livy looked at him, waiting for him to answer and ask the next logical question.

When he said nothing, she turned to Ranger Armstead, who gave a slight shake of his head. He seemed as frustrated with the man as Livy.

"When Mr. Miller brought back your bracelet with the new charm, did he say anything else about the incident?"

"No, nothing more about Dennis. And the only thing he said about the altercation was that I might have saved his life. After that he asked me about the trails in the valley. Which ones were crowded. Which were my favorites. I told him about the hike above Tuolumne Meadows. I recommended he take that one."

Her tone dropped off and she closed her eyes, trying not to see Mr. Miller's broken body splayed out on the ledge.

"And he took your advice…on the same day there just happened to be a fire—and *you* happened to be the one to find him, by pure accident." The investigator finally stepped back in…and his tone was snarky.

Livy's roller-coaster emotions finally exploded.

"Excuse me. What was your name and who are you?"

"My name is Aaron Garanetti… I'm the state fire inspector appointed by Representative Blankenship to investigate this situation."

"Well, Mr. Garanetti, what I find strange is that you think I would start a fire and risk getting caught in it, then risk my life again climbing down to rescue Mr. Miller. Why would I put myself or anyone else in that kind of danger?"

"You received a commendation yesterday. Some people might risk a lot for that kind of recognition."

Livy closed her eyes. This was impossible. Unbelievable.

"Yesterday a hero. Today an arsonist," she murmured, then shook her head in disbelief.

"We don't think you're an arsonist, Livy." Ranger Armstead sent a sharp glance toward the investigator. "But we have to explore all the possibilities, including the likelihood that you or Miller were targeted."

Targeted? They thought someone set the fire on the trail purposely to trap her and Mr. Miller. It was too much to consider. Too overwhelming.

Ignoring the investigator, she looked at Ranger Armstead. "Am I being fired?"

Her supervisor's jaw tightened. "Of course not. But…"

Livy tensed at the word.

Ranger Armstead continued, "Just to keep things low-key, we're putting you on light duties for now. We want you to stay down here in the valley until we find the arsonist."

Light duties. She didn't know what that meant and right now, she didn't care. All she wanted was to leave the room to get away from Inspector Garanetti's stony, suspicious gaze.

He asked her a few more questions. Was she sure she didn't notice anything before the fire? Any other suspicious activity? She really hadn't smelled the gasoline or heard anything that seemed out of place?

Livy did her best to answer, but she was still in too much shock to think clearly. She needed some space and time to get her bearings. She fumbled her way through, responding mostly with "I don't remember."

She was probably doing her case more harm than good, but she couldn't help it. She was completely blown away.

At last, the investigator released her. Rising, she nodded to Ranger Armstead and hurried out the door. She couldn't even look at the receptionist outside Armstead's office door.

Rushing past, she lunged outside and hurried down the walkway, determined to get to her car and go far away. Suddenly, Hayden Bryant stepped into her path.

She stopped abruptly and stared up at him. It was early. The autumn air was crisp. He had a blue knitted cap pulled down so low over his head that no black curls escaped it. Even this early, he had the dark shadow of a beard on his cheeks and jaw. It gave his appearance a dangerous air Livy found impossible to ignore. The naturally brooding set of his dark brows and eyes only added to that image.

Right now, his forehead was furrowed even more than usual. He folded his plaid-covered arms and nudged his chin back toward the office.

"Are they done with you?"

Caught off guard, Livy could only shrug. "I... I guess. I don't know—I..."

She floundered.

Hayden took her arm. "Come on. We're getting away from here."

His firm grip felt like the only stable thing in Livy's world. She leaned into him as he moved toward his truck.

He opened the passenger door, holding it open for her. She was about to step in, but a thought occurred to her. She halted. "Wait...how do you know about... their suspicions? That they were questioning me? Does every employee know?"

Hayden heaved a sigh. "If they don't, they soon will."

Livy sagged and was more thankful for his sturdy arm holding her up.

"Get in. You need something hot to drink."

She shook her head. "No... I can't go to the park restaurant. I can't face everyone. Not yet."

"I know. I'm taking you someplace else."

Numb with relief, Livy climbed inside. Hayden came around to get in the driver's seat, then started the engine and pulled out of the parking lot. He drove down the valley's main road, past the turnoff leading to the south entrance, and kept going, winding down the twisting, narrow road that followed the Merced River. Hayden never said a word, just drove silently. Livy stared at the sparkling river beside them and the cliffs on each side of the river valley.

She let her head fall back against the seat and closed her eyes. Inspector Garanetti's insinuating tone and hard features flashed through her mind. What was he probing for? And why, when she remembered something worth mentioning, did he abruptly clam up? Did he actually believe she had something to do with that fire or was he just looking for a scapegoat?

Panic ripped through her body, and she searched for breath between gasps. Without a word, Hayden pushed a button and the window beside her rolled down. Crisp, pine-scented air flowed over her.

She took in deep, gulping breaths. The scent, the sparkling river and the glorious granite cliffs on each side of her soothed her strained senses. She closed her eyes and let this wonderful place calm her frazzled nerves.

Hayden didn't speak. Soon they left the sharp twists and turns of the valley and drove away from the river. A small roadside café appeared in the distance. It was so small if you blinked, you'd miss it. But the parking lot was full of cars, a sign of good food and excellent service.

Hayden pulled in and parked. As the engine died down, he turned to look at her. "Are you ready to go inside?"

She nodded and gestured to the window. "Thanks for that. I needed it."

He shrugged. "Been there myself."

Punching the button, the window raised. He climbed out and Livy followed, lost in thought.

What did he mean? Hayden seemed fearless and invincible. She'd seen him climb cliffs others wouldn't dare. How could he possibly be susceptible to panic attacks like the one she'd felt coming on?

Puzzled, she trailed behind him as he led the way into the café. There was an empty booth in the corner, and he headed straight for it. Sliding into the bench seat, she settled herself and waited for the server to come by to take their order.

She was an older lady with a Southern twang. "Hey, Hayden. Haven't seen you in a while. Had a busy season in the park?"

"Yeah, long and busy."

"What can I get for you two?"

Livy ordered a hot chocolate and Hayden black coffee. He didn't speak again until Livy took the first sip of her drink.

Smiling, he handed her a napkin. "Here, dangerous arsonist. You have whipped cream on your upper lip."

Livy chuckled. She couldn't help it. Of all the things she expected him to say, that was the most surprising—but it was also powerfully reassuring. His tone, his smile, everything about him telegraphed kindness and seemed to put her situation in perspective. If Hayden didn't take the inspector's insinuations seriously, wouldn't others feel the same way?

She hoped so, because she couldn't seem to find her

way out of the maze of confusion. At least she wasn't about to have another panic attack. Not yet, anyway.

Hayden sipped his coffee, then met her gaze. "I asked Armstead to assign you to me until this is resolved. I have a number of climbing classes coming and tons of people signed up…not to mention my search and rescue duties if an emergency arises. I can use the help of a skilled climber."

Livy nodded. If being Hayden's sidekick for a few weeks was the worst she had to endure, she just might survive. Most of the single females in the park would envy her. Handsome, brooding Hayden Bryant sweeping in to rescue her was the stuff from a romance novel. But of course, a change in duties wasn't the only problem she faced. Livy's reputation and career were on the line—and Hayden stepping up, volunteering to help her, were his way of making it clear he was on her side. He was risking his own reputation by publicly supporting her. As soon as she remembered that, every romantic notion was quickly knocked out of her head. All she could feel was gratitude.

"Thank you for…finding me and bringing me here… for everything."

"No need to thank me. Anyone who knows you, knows you had nothing to do with the fire."

"Tell that to the investigator."

"Ignore him. He's probably looking for a promotion and believes a high-profile case will be his way up the ladder."

"But he was right. It seems suspicious. Like someone was trying to involve me. But how and, more importantly, why?"

"The how is easy. Do you have daily routine? Do you take that hike often?"

She nodded slowly. "I'd only been in Tuolumne a couple of days before then, but yes, I hiked that trail every day."

"There you go. You were predictable. All someone had to do was wait."

She gave him a rueful shake of her head. "I didn't make them wait long."

Hayden gave her a small smile. "No, you didn't. Now we have to ask why you were targeted in the first place."

She shook her head. "That investigator seemed to believe there was some other connection between me and Mr. Miller. I never saw the man before the day I broke up the disagreement between him and Dennis Ludlow."

"Ludlow was a problem for all of us. He applied for the rescue team, and I turned him down. His reputation preceded him."

"But it was my report about the altercation between him and Mr. Miller that got him fired and kicked out of the park."

Hayden's features were bland. "Don't feel too bad. It was bound to happen sooner or later. That guy is trouble."

Livy closed her eyes. "I wish I'd realized that before I tried to be his friend."

Hayden leaned back against the booth. "Don't tell me. He thought you wanted to be more than a friend."

Livy's shoulders sagged, hunching forward a little in embarrassment. "Everyone disliked him so much, I felt sorry for him. I just wanted to encourage him, maybe lift him up."

Leaning forward again, Hayden placed his elbows on the table with a rueful shake of his head. "Just trying to save the world, one idiot at a time."

Livy wanted to protest what seemed like a jaded attitude, but she couldn't. Hayden was right. She had wanted to help, and she'd let that instinct push her further than was wise. She should have steered clear of Dennis Ludlow.

"Looks like I'm the only idiot this time," she murmured.

Hayden nodded his head in agreement and Livy looked away. She wished he hadn't been so quick to concur.

"Wait a minute, is that the connection the investigator was trying to make? That you and Miller were more than casual acquaintances?"

She nodded. "He kept pointing out how my meetings with Mr. Miller were too coincidental—that I just happened to be there to break up the fight with Dennis, and then later, that I was the one who found him right before he died." She shrugged. "The scary part is…he was right."

A shiver ran through her. "When I first walked up to them, I heard Dennis tell Mr. Miller he was watching him. At the time, I thought he was talking about watching him in the store and seeing Mr. Miller break the snow globe."

She looked up. "But now I'm wondering if Dennis meant he'd been watching him before. I'd never met Mr. Miller prior to that day—but that doesn't mean that he and Dennis were strangers, too. Maybe there was history there that I didn't know about."

Hayden's dark gaze searched her face. "You mean he could have been watching Miller the day of the fire."

"No, I saw Dennis pack everything into his car and leave the park."

Hayden shook his head. "You saw him leave the employee complex. That doesn't mean he actually left the park."

Livy nodded slowly. "If he was following Mr. Miller, then he could have poured the gas and set the sparkler sticks after I arrived."

She inhaled slowly to calm her spiraling nerves. "I know Dennis had problems, but I still can't believe he would try to murder anyone."

Hayden sighed. "Maybe the fire wasn't meant to kill him. Maybe it was meant as a warning and got out of hand. After all, it wasn't the fire itself that killed Miller—he died after hitting his head when he fell, right? Dennis lived in this area all his life. From what he wrote on his application, he knew this park as well as you or I. If he saw you hiking after Miller, he might have thought you'd be able to get the man off the trail via the ridge."

She nodded slowly. "I thought the same thing that day, but Mr. Miller had already gone far beyond the cut-off. I had to follow him. But I still can't believe Dennis would take that kind of risk. He loves Yosemite and knows the fire danger right now."

"Did you see anyone else near there?"

"No. In fact, I was shocked to see Mr. Miller's car in the parking lot. It was late in the day and there was no traffic on the pass, absolutely none. Oh…except that guy on the lookout who reported the fire. I forgot all about him when I talked to the inspector."

Hayden froze. "What guy? As far as I know the only report that came in was from you."

She shrugged. "Well… I thought he was reporting the fire. He was parked on the lookout, you know, the one on the curve that faces the valley beyond the trail. He had binoculars and was watching us. He got into his car and drove away, so I just assumed he was hurrying off to find help."

"Did you get a good look at the guy?"

"No, but I don't think it was Dennis, if that's what you're thinking. It certainly wasn't his car. He had a clunky red car. The one on the ridge was white—a little economy-size car."

"He could have switched vehicles."

She huffed. "You're determined to pin this on Dennis, aren't you? Why would he risk starting a fire just to threaten Mr. Miller?"

Hayden shook his head, and his brow furrowed into a serious frown. "I don't know, but Dennis is involved. I can feel it in my gut. If you want to get to the bottom of this, you're going to have to stop looking at the world through your rose-colored glasses. Refusing to see what's really going on just might get you killed."

Hayden studied Livy across the table. By the look on her face, he was pretty sure his statement offended her. But she didn't argue…at least not yet. Color was returning to her cheeks. The shock she'd experienced from dealing with the investigator this morning was wearing off. That was a good sign. He had no doubt that when she was more like her old self, they'd revisit this conversation.

She'd probably scold him for criticizing her outlook. He knew that it was important to her to view the world in a positive light. But sooner or later, she had to realize that things didn't always turn out for the best. If she wanted to get through this in one piece, she had to come to that understanding. Looking for the good in everyone wasn't going to get her the answers she needed to survive.

Dale had informed Hayden that he'd contacted the national park system's investigators. Their own people were already on the way. The only reason Dale had let Garanetti interview Livy this morning was to get the visiting politician off his back. But from what Livy had said, Garanetti had asked all the wrong things. His questions were more about her connections to Miller than the fire. It was almost as if he wanted answers to something other than the cause of the blaze.

Pulling out his phone, he typed Garanetti's name into a search bar. A picture popped up of the investigator standing next to the politician who had attended Livy's award ceremony yesterday. The headline of the article read "Blankenship's Grassroots Effort Wins."

Garanetti had worked on Todd Blankenship's campaign. Even Hayden hadn't expected the answer to be so obvious.

Shaking his head, he held the phone up for Livy to see. "Recognize him?"

She studied the picture and article, then looked at him. "Garanetti campaigned for Blankenship and got the job he wanted. Politicians give their supporters jobs. That's how it works."

"Yes, and sometimes the supporters do the bidding of their sponsor, too—even if that means trashing someone's reputation to give their sponsor an advantage."

"Maybe. But what could I do to help or hurt a state representative? I'm just a second-year ranger. What can I do to him or anyone else, for that matter?"

"I don't think they saw you as a threat. It sounds like Garanetti was trying to find out what you knew about Dennis and his connections to Miller. Also, I don't think Garanetti expected you to stand up for yourself—or that you would have friends willing to help you."

She heaved a sigh and looked away. "Don't get me wrong but that doesn't make sense either."

"What?"

She sighed. "Why, Hayden? If this is some conspiracy, with someone powerful enough to manipulate a state representative, it could impact Ranger Armstead and you, too. If they think I'm guilty, defending me might look bad for you two. Why are you sticking your necks out to help me?"

"I can't speak for Dale but I'm doing it because it *does* seem like a conspiracy." He gave a brief, frustrated shrug of his shoulders. "Life deals out enough tragedy without people making it more difficult. Accidents happen and people die. One minute you're on top of the world. The next you're flattened beneath it." He looked up and fixed his gaze on her. "You learned this morning just how heavy the world can be."

She swallowed and frowned. His answer didn't seem to please her. Was she hoping his reasons for helping her were more personal? He was treading deep water with Livy's naive emotions.

Whatever thoughts caused the frown, she pushed them away and said, "What you're suggesting is they think I'm an easy target. Just a pawn in a bigger plan. But for what purpose? What can I possibly do?"

"That's what we have to figure out. But believe me, if Boyd Goldberg is involved, there is a plan."

Her lips parted in surprise. She had pretty, full, pink lips. The kind that invited a second look. Hayden had to force his gaze away, especially after her blue eyes widened in surprise.

"Boyd Goldberg...you think he's involved, too?"

Her expression and her tone telegraphed her disbelief. Gritting his teeth, Hayden realized he'd let too much slip. That was what losing his focus did. He hadn't meant to tell her about Boyd, but he'd gotten distracted. At least, he hadn't wanted to bring him up just now. Hayden knew expressing his opinions about Boyd out loud would sound over-the-top. To someone who didn't know their backstory, it would sound like he was just making something up about a celebrity. And to someone who *did* know their history...well, it would probably sound like he was looking for an excuse to go after the man.

But Livy would need to know what was going on so she could protect herself, which meant that he had to tell her the whole sordid story...and risk losing her trust. He struggled to put years of suspicion into words.

"Look, I know it sounds wild, but I think he might be involved. Yesterday I was watching your ceremony."

"You were there?"

"Yeah, I was. I wanted to support you."

A slight smile played about her lips. "Thanks. That was kind."

That small smile did something to his insides. The feeling, whatever it was, needed to be stopped, unrelentingly squashed before it grew. "There was nothing kind about my actions," he insisted. "First responders need recognition. What you did took courage. I was there to show respect for that."

The pleased light in her features bled away. Hayden tried not to notice. "Anyway, while I was standing there, Boyd's wife came up to me and told me about the accusations against you."

"She knew about it before I did?"

"Yes. Even before I did. If that doesn't create ideas about a plan being set in motion, then I don't know what does."

"How did she know?"

"Apparently she overheard Blankenship telling Boyd."

Livy shook her head, looking confused. "Why would Blankenship talk to him? Is Boyd a supporter, too?"

"I don't know but I imagine, if we look hard enough, we'll find a connection."

She eyed him skeptically. "Paulette just walked up and started telling you her husband's private conversations?"

"Paulette and I…we have history."

"She was your fiancée—I remember hearing about that. The two of you got a lot of press back then, especially when the relationship ended."

Hayden fought to hold back a wince. He'd wondered

how much she knew about that, had even let himself hope that she might not know. She didn't seem like the type to read tabloids. But apparently, she'd heard all about it. Probably from the work grapevine she had worried about when he first met her this morning.

"She left you for Boyd, but you're still friends?" Livy asked.

The doubt in her voice signaled her disbelief, the exact response he'd hoped to avoid.

"No, actually, we haven't talked in years. But yesterday she approached me with an apology. She said she was sorry for the way things happened."

Hayden was more than uncomfortable discussing this. He rarely discussed his life with anyone, and he wouldn't be talking now, but Livy needed to understand. He needed to make her see how dangerous Boyd could be.

"She seemed…" He paused, not sure how to describe what he'd sensed in Paulette. "I don't know. Sincere maybe, and definitely sorry. Then she warned me about what was going to happen to you."

Livy stared at him for a long while. "After three years, your ex-fiancée walks up to you and apologizes for dumping you, then in the next breath betrays her husband's privacy by revealing a conversation he had that she overheard…and you trust her?" She gave a small shake of her head. "And you say *I* look at the world through rose-colored glasses."

Hayden shifted in his seat. "Obviously, Paulette was telling the truth. Everything happened exactly as she said. Garanetti is trying to tie you to the fire."

She studied him again. For someone with a naive outlook, she certainly had a penetrating gaze. It felt like she was looking right through him to the core of his being.

"Did you believe the apology? If, like you said, there's some grand plan in motion, she could be a vital part of it."

Hayden tensed before releasing a breath. "Unfortunately, I think she realized partway through the convo that Boyd had manipulated her. It was a shock to her."

Those pretty pink lips parted again. Then she pressed her hands to her face and shook her head. "The world you live in is a sad, bitter place."

He was silent for a long while. "Perhaps. But I think it just became your world, too."

She tilted her head back until it rested against the back of the booth. "This is all too much. I can't deal with your…past. Let's go back to the beginning where it all started with the fire and Dennis. He said he was leaving the park."

"Saying something and doing it are two different things."

"I watched him pack everything and drive away. A friend told me she saw him leaving through the south gate."

Hayden shrugged. "He could have changed cars and come back in a different vehicle. That would make sense, especially if he was planning to commit arson. He wouldn't want to be in a recognizable car."

She gave him a negative shake. "Fair enough. But who has that kind of money to throw around? He wasn't exactly working for top dollar here. Could he really afford two cars?"

Hayden shrugged. The answer seemed obvious to

him. The car could have been provided by someone else—someone with deep pockets. Boyd had his fingers in all kinds of financial deals. He stared at Livy, waiting for her to draw the same conclusion. At first, she refused to meet his stare.

Finally, she threw her hands up. "All right, you win. Boyd Goldberg could be manipulating the situation. But if there's some sinister backstory between Mr. Miller and Dennis—and Boyd Goldberg, too, apparently— then that means Mr. Miller was caught up in something nefarious. He was so kind. I just can't believe he would be involved in something illegal."

Hayden shook his head. "People aren't always what they seem, Livy. Maybe he was putting on a good act."

Her eyes widened again, and she was silent for a long while. "I can't believe you'd jump to that conclusion." She shook her head. "You are a hard man, Hayden Bryant."

His jaw tightened. "Maybe so. But I'm the one standing beside you right now."

Her shoulders slumped, and she looked away. "That's true."

The silence stretched out again. At last, Hayden relented. "Look, I'm not saying Mr. Miller is guilty of anything. I'm just saying we have to look at things from all angles. None of this makes sense. Why would anyone want to involve you? And if Miller was as innocent as you think, why would Dennis be following him? There must be some connection, and we have to look for it from every direction."

She nodded. "You forgot the fight in the store. Mr. Miller was connected to Dennis through that."

"And there's the fact that Boyd knew about the investigator's intentions long before me. I was the lead authority on that rescue. If there was an investigation, I should have been informed immediately...and been a part of the interrogation."

He shook his head. "It's like some program is running in the background, using up our batteries but we don't know what it is. We need to find it and shut it down."

She seemed to come around and gave a slow nod. "So, what do we do now?"

"We tell Dale our suspicions and then let our guys from the Investigative Services Branch do their job. They handle all crimes in the national parks and from what I've heard, they're the best."

She was silent for a long moment. Then she straightened her shoulders and met his gaze. "You're right. It's time to meet this head-on."

THREE

Slightly surprised by her quick agreement, Hayden rose and placed some money on the table for their drinks. "My treat."

Livy thanked him and headed for the glass doors of the café. She hurried to his parked truck. Now that she'd made up her mind to act, she seemed pretty determined to move forward. Quite a change from the stunned woman she'd been on the drive here. Hayden was impressed.

He unlocked the truck and they climbed in. They'd only gone a few miles when he noticed a white car behind them moving up quickly. The driver, a man wearing a baseball cap pulled down low and dark glasses, was going way too fast for the narrow mountain road curves. Determined to let the dangerous driver pass, Hayden pumped the brakes and purposely slowed down. The driver slowed down, too.

Frowning, Hayden sped up. The driver sped up to match them, coming so close, Hayden couldn't see the front end of the car in his rearview mirror.

Murmuring his frustration, Hayden pumped the

brakes again, warning the diver off. He backed off but not far enough to make Hayden comfortable.

"What color was that car you saw on the ridge?"

"White."

"You said it was a smaller economy car, right? Did it look like the one behind us?"

She turned and studied the car following too close for comfort.

"It may be it. I don't know for sure. I didn't get a good look at the car or the driver. Isn't he too close?"

"Yes, he is." Hayden pumped the brakes and slowed down even further. The driver followed suit, backing off at least fifty feet.

"Well, that's better but he's still too close." Hayden studied the car. The windows were tinted very dark, in defiance of California vehicle codes. The driver was sitting far back in his seat so they couldn't see his face.

Livy turned around to watch the car. "I don't recognize him or the car. I've seen Dennis's car skulking around me enough to know it by sight. That's not it."

"Not the one that he wants people to associate with him, anyway," Hayden countered.

They hit a straightaway, so Hayden sped up. The powerful engine of the truck had an advantage over the smaller car when they were climbing. But as soon as they hit the curves, Hayden was forced to slow down, and the little car rapidly gained on them.

They traveled out of the populated areas, headed for the twisting curves of the narrow road above the sparkling Merced River. The little car followed close behind.

Suddenly, up ahead was a turnoff. A barely marked fire trail wove its way up the hill. Hayden swerved onto it so quickly, the truck tilted on two wheels. He gunned the accelerator and sped up the dirt path, kicking up stones and dirt behind him.

"Now we'll know for sure if he's following us."

The path climbed up the side of the hill, kicking up so much dust, they couldn't see if the car was still behind them. At last, the dirt path curved around the mountain, winding its way to a high peak through a series of switchbacks.

Hayden took the curves for another twenty minutes, climbing the hill. He pumped the brakes, slowing on another curve. "This is only going to lead us higher into the backcountry. We can't just keep driving."

They came to a wide spot in the road. He stopped so quickly, dirt and pebbles blew over them and sprinkled on the roof. He made a three-point turn on the narrow path and blocked it. If the car had followed them, the driver would have no place to go. The other car wouldn't be able to go around them, and it didn't have the power to push them off the road. Hayden's larger truck had the advantage on the skinny path with the mountain on one side and the sloping hillside on the other.

The little car came around the corner and skidded to a stop. It slid sideways before stopping completely, still rocking back and forth in the middle of the road. Neither vehicle moved for a long while.

"What if he just backs down the mountain?" Livy murmured, almost as if she was afraid to speak.

"He can't back all the way down. There's no way he can get away...unless he goes over the side and down that slope."

As if hearing Hayden's words, the driver of the car

backed up. Then he spun to the right and drove straight off the road. Livy screamed as the little car went flying through the air. It flew four feet straight down to a flat plateau, hit the ground and bounced with a bone-jarring bump. Apparently, the car was too old for airbags because they didn't release, at least not that Hayden could tell.

After a moment, the little car's engine revved. The wheels spun and kicked dirt behind it, sending pine needles and dust up into the air. The car moved down the slope, dodging trees and rocks until it disappeared behind the shrub oaks at the base of the hill.

Hayden mumbled his frustration, then gunned his accelerator, driving the truck over to the shoulder to look down to the place where the driver had left the road. The rear bumper of the car had caught on the rocks of the precipice and had fallen off. It rocked back and forth precariously on the edge.

For one heartbeat, Hayden considered following the driver truck over the edge. Instead, he pounded the steering wheel, then slammed the door open and ran to look down.

Livy followed him. They stared at the tracks of dirt the car ploughed through the golden weeds on the hillside. They couldn't see the vehicle, except for an occasional white flash moving through the trees. But they could hear the motor revving and sputtering, trying to die out. His engine was threatening to stop running—but it hadn't quit yet.

"Where can he go?"

Hayden shook his head. "I don't know. I suppose if

he doesn't get stuck and he can keep the engine running, he'll hit another fire trail somewhere."

They listened as the engine continued to splutter and rev. At one point, metal crunched, as if it had hit something hard. But then the engine put-putted back to life and the sound moved farther and farther away.

Hayden studied the trail the car had left, the deep skid marks, and the zigzags down the slope.

Livy shook her head. "He must be desperate to take that risk."

"Or he's unbalanced."

Livy nodded slowly. "When he turned the car to go over the edge, he came pretty close to my side of the truck. I glimpsed his profile. It reminded me of Dennis."

Hayden studied her concerned features before he turned and headed back to the truck. "Come on. We need to get back and report this."

Dale's voice sounded confident over the phone. "The folks from the National Park Investigative Services Branch just arrived. After they get settled, I'll fill them in. I can't wait to get their take on this. I don't trust that investigator from the state."

It was exactly what Hayden needed to hear from his supervisor. When they returned to the park yesterday, they went straight to Armstead. But the usually calm supervisor seemed overwhelmed. The situation was morphing into something beyond his scope of experience. He had been more flustered than Hayden had ever seen him. But this morning, he sounded confident.

Hayden needed him to be confident because he still felt like things were slipping out of control. The whole encounter with the driver the previous day had shaken Hayden more than he wanted to admit. Had it really been Dennis? If so, what had he been after when he'd followed them—and what motivation moved him to drive off the road like that?

"I let Garanetti push me around yesterday to keep the peace with Representative Blankenship, but now that our own investigators have arrived, they'll take over. I don't trust Garanetti. I'm sure he and Blankenship have an agenda. I just can't figure out what it is."

Hayden was glad to hear Dale confirm his own suspicions. All yesterday afternoon and last night, he wondered if he was allowing his past to color his perspective on Livy's situation. It was good to hear Dale, a man whose judgment he trusted, sharing the same doubts.

Dale's tone was low. "You know... I put Livy on special duty to protect her as much as anything else. I know I can trust you to shut Garanetti down if he gets too close to her."

"You can count on it. Any news on the car that followed us?"

"Not yet. I've put out a bulletin to our rangers and local law enforcement with a description. It's too bad you two didn't get a license plate. It might have made finding the car easier. I also contacted the National Guard. They agreed to send a helicopter to do a fly-over. It'll be taking off in about an hour. We're short-handed with Jenna and her husband out on parental leave. It took me a while to get a crew lined up, but a team will be heading over there first thing tomorrow to see if they can find any evidence on the ground. There's a chance they might even find the car itself, if it ended up breaking down. But your guess is probably right. More than likely, the driver came across a fire trail and followed it out."

"Probably."

"By the way, I pulled Dennis Ludlow's employment records. Besides applying to search and rescue, he applied to the fire team. According to his application, all he ever wanted was to fight wildland fires."

Hayden digested the information. "So, he's a bit of a firebug."

Armstead chuckled. "Ever know a firefighter who wasn't fascinated by fire? Good thing most of them have a healthy respect for the damage it causes."

"Yeah. I'm telling you, Dale. The way that driver drove off the side of the mountain was reckless. He had absolutely no concern for his own welfare, let alone anyone else's. That action has me worried."

"Me, too. Especially with a park full of climbing enthusiasts."

"Speaking of climbers, I've got a class lining up for their first session. I better go."

"I'll keep you posted…and Hayden? Take care of our girl. She's got the makings of a great ranger. I don't want to lose her over this incident."

"Will do."

Hayden ended the call and studied "our girl." Livy stood a few feet away, reading something on her phone and smiling. She wore close-fitting clothes appropriate for climbing, including a good pair of shoes. A climber's shoes were essential, and he approved of the brand she chose. But there was more to appreciate. Her puffy vest was a pretty shade of blue that matched her eyes.

Normally Hayden wouldn't have noticed that kind of thing, but her blue gaze jumped right out and demanded attention.

"What's got you smiling?"

She looked up, and those eyes took his breath away. They almost sparkled, full of joy. She held up the phone, and he glimpsed a picture of a newborn swaddled in a white hospital blanket.

"My goddaughter is finally here. Isn't she precious?"

"Jenna delivered her baby?"

"Yes, she arrived early this morning."

"Raul must be relieved."

She giggled. "He's so relieved, he's acting like a goof."

Hayden laughed, too. "Yeah. I figured. Mr. Too Cool for school was gonna turn out to be one of those silly dads."

Livy laughed again. Hayden decided he liked the sound of her laughter.

"Jenna has already said she's going to have to be the disciplinarian. She knew Raul would turn into putty the first time he saw his daughter."

Hayden grabbed a climbing rope off the back of his truck and looped it tighter. "Now that you've talked to them, what do they say about your situation?"

Her features turned somber. "I didn't tell them. I'm not going to spoil this special time for them with worries about my...situation. There'll be plenty of time for that later."

He paused. "That's a really kind thing to do, Livy."

She lifted one shoulder in a shrug. "Jenna's always been there for me, through all my hard times. It's the least I can do."

All her hard times? He'd always pictured Livy as having the perfect life. He hadn't really thought she had challenges, especially given her Pollyanna attitude. He thought her naivete came from having lived a sheltered existence. Maybe he was wrong about that.

Frowning, Hayden concentrated on the students lining up for his class. This was a group of intermediate climbers, looking to reach their next level. Hayden was going to work with them on a small climb. It was preparation for a more strenuous hike and climb behind El Capitan that was planned for the next day. All the participants thought today's lesson was about mastering techniques, but in Hayden's mind, it was for him to determine if they were ready for tomorrow.

He introduced himself and Livy, then jumped straight into a discussion of equipment. Most instructors assumed intermediate climbers knew enough about equipment already and glossed over those details. But given Hayden's background, he never skipped a review of life-saving tools.

He asked Livy to model his explanations. She stepped into the safety harness, pulled it up and belted it at her waist. Hayden couldn't stop the flashback of a few short days ago when she'd completed the same action on the mountainside while he was suspended over Miller's body. She looked up and met his gaze. That bright joy that her eyes had held just a minute ago was gone. Now they were filled with sadness and Hayden knew she was remembering that day, too.

Taking a deep breath, he focused on the group in front of him. Today was about best practices. Unlike him, they had no idea how bad things could go. After the initial review, Hayden continued to talk. Livy went around the group, checking knots and belay plates, and locking carabiners.

It went well, at first—most of the climbers were eager to cooperate and excited for the day's climb. But it only took one person to make a situation turn sour. Hayden had taught enough classes to recognize a troublemaker when he saw one. As Livy approached him, one tall man folded his arms. He had a square jaw and shoulders that looked like a bodybuilder's. Hayden tensed when the man completely ignored Livy. Not backing down, she planted herself right in front of him and requested him, in a loud voice, to show her his knots and carabiners.

"I know how to tie knots."

"I'm sure you do. But you won't climb that cliff until I examine your equipment. Or, at least, you won't climb with this class."

Hayden ducked his head to hide his smile. Livy wasn't lacking in courage or grit. That much was for sure. Huffing, the troublemaker tossed his belay plate at her. Livy deftly caught the heavy metal clutch called a GriGri, and turned it over several times, carefully examining it. Not showing any hesitation, she stepped toward the taller man and tugged on the figure-eight knots attached to the waist of his harness.

When she was done, she tossed the plate back to him with less force than he'd sent it to her. It sailed toward him, and he grabbed at it, but it hit his chest a bit hard. He flinched and his lips tightened, but he made no comment.

Hayden looked down to hide his smile again as Livy joined him at the front of the class. With the smile wiped away, he looked up and he began his lecture. "As you know, our class today is in preparation for our climb tomorrow. The cliff I've chosen to tackle in the morning is challenging, but it offers us one of the best views of the backcountry."

Hayden smiled. "However, it comes after a long four-hour hike that requires stamina. If you haven't acclimated, you might want to wait and tackle this climb later in the week."

He was really hoping Ron, the troublemaker, would take his advice and reconsider, especially after the man held back, arms folded, while the others crowded forward to take their turn climbing the easier rock wall in front of them.

Hayden stayed on the ground, giving instructions to the climbers as, one by one, they scaled the cliff. He was able to watch their progress and give tips while Livy belayed. She attached their ropes to the plate on her harness and monitored the safety rope, removing the slack as they ascended and releasing it as they descended.

Everyone went up with few problems except Ron. Just as Hayden suspected he would, he stalked forward, hooked Livy's rope to his GriGri, spun the locking carabiner closed and attacked the cliff, never once acknowledging Livy. He didn't even bother to dip his fingers in the bag of chalk attached to his waist. Chalk was essential to prevent sweaty fingers from slipping, especially on a warm day like today. Ron just scaled up the wall, using his brute strength and not his brains. Just the kind of action that would cause problems. The cliff was easy to scale at the bottom, but the top was slick granite with few good toe- or fingerholds. If Ron didn't slow down and plan his ascent, he was headed for a mistake.

Near the top, it was clear that Ron was tiring. Even from fifty feet below, they could hear heavy panting as he searched in vain for his next toehold. He couldn't find a good place, and Hayden let him flounder.

At last, Ron's left toe slipped off the nub of granite on which it was balanced. He hung by his fingertips for a moment before he slid down the cliff face. Livy locked the belay rope against her body and held it steady. The friction of the GriGri slowed Ron's momentum as she carefully lowered him all the way to the ground.

When both feet were firmly down on the ground, Ron leaned into the granite wall and closed his eyes. He would surely have scrapes and bruises to show for his actions. But now that he was safe, Hayden had no intention of staying silent.

"Aren't you glad Livy put a second pair of eyes on your equipment?" Hayden's tone was icy. After losing his best friend, he had no patience for the careless attitude the man exhibited toward basic safety guidelines. Not to mention, he was incredibly rude.

"If you'd missed a knot, or had a bad plate or carabiner, your brief climb could have been the end of you. Never treat your equipment so thoughtlessly…or your partners. A little extra consideration might save your life."

Not even pausing to see the man's reaction, Hayden unhooked the rope from the belay plate on Livy's harness and began untying the knots. He turned to face the small class.

"We'll meet at the trailhead for Mist Trail at eight o'clock tomorrow morning. See you all there."

Some of the class departed. Others remained to talk to Hayden. Ron walked past him without a word. Livy silently picked up the spare ropes and loaded them into the truck. It took a while to gather all their equipment. Livy did most of the work, as Hayden was occupied answering the climbers' questions. It bothered him how they still treated him like a celebrity, many of them asking about notable climbs he'd done years before. Didn't they realize that he'd left that life behind? Now he was all about saving lives.

At last, the students were gone. Livy unbuckled her harness, let it slide to the ground and stepped out of it. "Thanks for that."

Surprised, he turned to her. "For what?"

"Letting me handle Ron's rope. You can't talk to people like that. Sometimes you just have to show them you can do the job."

Hayden laughed, but it wasn't a pleasant sound. "I wanted to show him, all right. Guys like that shouldn't be climbing. He's an accident waiting to happen."

"Probably…and he wasn't just overconfident. It was almost like he was trying to… I don't know…show his disapproval of me. Do you think the rumor mill started and he knows that I'm under suspicion of…something?"

Hayden chuckled again. "'Something' is right. Garanetti is reaching for straws. But like I told you, the entire park probably knows. Bad news travels like wildfire."

She shook her head. "Really? You had to use that expression?"

He gave her a slight smile and shrugged. "Sorry. It seemed appropriate."

She tossed her harness onto the front seat of the truck and climbed in.

Hayden started the engine. "You know I'm right. You can't stop people from talking. That's why it's best to meet gossip head-on—reshape the narrative."

She didn't answer and soon enough, he was pulling into the parking lot of the main store. He looked at Livy. "Now is just as good a time as any to face the questions. I think you'll find most people—at least your coworkers—more supportive than judgmental. Come on. I'll buy you another drink."

Her smile was slow and somewhat rueful. "Thanks, but I'm not ready to talk about it yet. I'm going to hide out at home a little while longer. I'll see you tomorrow."

She climbed out of his truck and walked to her car. Hayden watched her go. He felt sorry for her. She didn't deserve the drama that had already started heading her way. Curiosity could sometimes be invasive and going from hero to perceived villain was a fast downhill journey. She didn't deserve that.

But since when was life fair?

Shaking his head, he walked into the refreshment area. It was busy and full of people. He saw a couple of his students. After waving, he spoke to the server behind the counter.

"Hey, Lisa. Got any of my favorite tuna sandwiches? I didn't see them in the case."

"We ran out. I was just headed to the back to make some more. If you can wait a few, I'll have one ready for you in ten."

"Sure. Take your time."

He grabbed a juice box and slogged it down. Then he strolled around the store. His thoughts traveled back to something Livy had said. Ron *had* acted strange, like he had an agenda besides attending the class. Short of saying the words out loud, he did everything he could to show disrespect for Livy. The whole situation rubbed Hayden the wrong way.

Was he being paranoid again and letting the situation ignite his imagination?

Sighing, he stopped at the window to study the patio area. Every table was full of bystanders sitting on nearby walls and fences, waiting for seats. In one corner, Boyd was holding court. It shouldn't have surprised Hayden. Boyd always managed to be where crowds gathered. At the busy lunch patio. Lecture areas. Campfire get-togethers. Boyd always had to be the center of attention.

He looked the same. He had on a long-sleeved dark sweater. His brown hair was tousled in a studied kind of way, more Hollywood than natural. Hayden knew for a fact that Boyd paid close attention to his looks, for all that he tried to make himself look windblown and natural. He had a slightly rounded face with a prominent chin and ski-slope nose. Hayden supposed he was good-looking, attractive enough to catch Paulette's attention. But for Hayden there was always something behind Boyd's eyes, something sharp and clever and mean, like Boyd knew something no one else knew and gloried in his superiority. It made the man ugly to him in a way that no amount of pleasant features or careful styling could fix. But apparently, Hayden was the only one put off by the man's manipulative air.

Even today, Boyd had a crowd around him. At least fifteen people surrounded his table, and he seemed to be telling stories. Every so often, the crowd would laugh or clap. Boyd was certainly in his element.

Hayden wondered what Boyd would do if he broke up his little show. Maybe it would be a good thing to let Boyd know he was watching him. Gritting his teeth, Hayden walked toward the back door before he could change his mind.

Boyd spied Hayden the minute he entered the patio area. A smile that Hayden could only describe as sly slid over Boyd's features.

"Look who decided to join us," he said, leaning back in his chair.

Hayden stopped a few feet away. "Hello, Boyd."

Boyd grinned and looked around the group. "Friends, I'm sure some of you will remember Hayden Bryant. Once upon a time, he was one of the world's leading climbers."

Hayden gritted his teeth at the phrasing, carefully chosen to make it clear that Hayden was a has-been. But rather than rising to the bait, he smiled and nodded. "Yeah. I still hold some world records...like the fastest free climb of El Capitan."

Boyd's smile faded but only for a moment. That small moment was enough for Hayden.

"Ah yes," he said with that same oily smile. "The record I'm here to break."

The crowd around them tittered with quickly suppressed laughter. Hayden didn't recognize any of the people. They were young and all-new to Hayden. That didn't surprise him much. The fans Boyd collected in the past were groupies trying to get close to someone famous.

Hayden smiled, too. "Congratulations. I heard you've been chosen to head up a new climbing school."

"I have. We're going to be neighbors. I'll be working out of Hetch Hetchy."

Hayden nodded. "With a program like that to put together, I would have thought you'd be too busy to train for a climb like El Capitan."

"I always have time to train. Unlike you, I never let my climbing instincts lapse."

Hayden shook his head at the dig. If he'd ever wondered if Boyd had changed, this conversation had assured him he had not.

"Well, Boyd, I just came to wish you the best on your attempt. It's going to be tough. You're not as young as you used to be."

Boyd's comfortable smile faded. "Don't worry about me, Hayden. I'm as fit as ever."

His tone was hard and Hayden realized he'd hit a sensitive spot with his old rival. "That's good. I'm not sure I'd attempt that climb again." Seeing no need to continue the conversation any further, Hayden shrugged. "Well, like I said. I wish you the best."

Boyd didn't reply, so Hayden nodded and walked back to the store counter to wait for his sandwich. Once inside he paused and looked back. Boyd was laughing again and gesturing to the crowd, probably saying something derogatory about Hayden. But Hayden didn't care what those silly kids thought of him. He had learned what he came to find out.

There was a new, sharp edge to Boyd. He was worried about something and Hayden suspected the least of his worries was the climb on El Capitan.

He started to turn away. Just then, Ron came from behind the building and joined the crowd. Boyd motioned to a man sitting next to him. The man rose and Ron took the seat right beside Boyd.

Gritting his teeth, Hayden spun and headed straight for Dale's office. He didn't trust Boyd and the fact that his annoying class attendee held a special place in Boyd's estimation was a red flag. He needed to speak to his supervisor about his concerns ASAP.

Before he reached his car, his cell phone rang. It was Livy.

"Hello?"

"Hayden, I—I need your help. Someone broke into my place and tore everything up. My house is—destroyed! I don't know what to do!"

FOUR

Livy stood outside her cabin in the employee complex. She couldn't stay inside and look at the slashed cushions, overturned bureaus and dumped-out drawers strewn on the floor. Whoever had picked the lock—and it was picked not broken—had done a thorough, destructive job of searching her home. But what were they looking for?

She shivered. The cold, late, autumn afternoon was doing nothing to ease her out of her shock. She took several deep breaths to calm down, but it didn't help. Whoever was behind this had done a professional job of wrecking her home and invading her privacy. This was supposed to be her safe place, the place where she came to lick her wounds and strengthen herself to go out into the world again. But that sense of sanctuary was ruined now.

She tried to get a grip, to pull herself together. After all, it had been less than two weeks since she had just saved the park from what could have been a serious fire and held a dying man's hand. Surely, she could get through this.

But her training and muscle memory took over in

that situation. After it was over, she melted into a puddle. Then she came home to her safe place and gathered her strength. But home wasn't safe anymore and right now, she couldn't even breathe.

Hayden drove up in his truck and flew out the door. Livy didn't hesitate. She needed to soak up some of his strength. She ran into his arms. But this time, he didn't wrap her in safety like he had on the cliff. He grabbed both her arms in a firm grip and held her slightly apart from him.

If he'd just put his arms around her, she might be able to breathe, but he kept her back enough to look her over, scanning for injuries.

"Are you all right?"

She felt the prick of hot tears and desperately fought them. Dropping her forehead against his chest, she shook her head. "If you mean, am I hurt—no, I am not. But I'm not all right either."

Gripping her arms, he pushed her farther away again and ducked his head to see her downward gaze. "Look at me, Livy."

All she wanted was to burrow into his chest again. If he'd just hold her…

But he didn't and at last, she raised her gaze. One solitary tear slipped down her cheek and she swiped it away.

"Did they take anything?"

She shook her head. "Not that I could see. Nothing but my peace of mind."

His jaw tightened. "You can get that back."

She looked away. He didn't know how hard she'd fought to earn that peace, to wake up every morning, knowing that she could get through this day and the next and the next. He had no clue how fragile her hold on life was. And now, given his current response, she feared if he knew, he wouldn't respect her.

Taking a deep breath, she stepped back out of his grip. Wrapping her arms around herself, she turned to look at her cabin. But she couldn't suppress another shiver.

"Let me get you a blanket."

"I have my coat in my car. I'll get it."

Turning her back to him, she forced herself to walk toward the driveway and finally, finally remembered to say her prayer. Step by step, word by word, she felt her courage growing. She didn't find peace, but she gained control.

More cars pulled up. Ranger Armstead climbed out of one, followed by two men and one woman. Armstead hurried to her side. Her supervisor did what she wished Hayden had done. He hugged her.

"Are you all right, Livy?"

"I'm fine." She glanced at Hayden. "I lost it for a moment or two but I'm okay now."

Armstead kept one arm around her as he introduced the others. "These are the national park's investigators, Livy. Mitch Pruitt is the lead. Larry Gault is the forensic specialist, and this is Special Agent Maggie Torres."

They nodded to Livy before Pruitt took charge. He was a short man but there was no mistaking his authoritative voice. "I'm sorry we're meeting under these conditions but that seems to be our lot."

Maggie Torres gave a little laugh. She was a redhead with her long hair twisted in a bun at the back of her head. She smiled and Livy couldn't miss the smattering of freckles across her nose.

She scrunched one shoulder in agreement. "You got that right, boss."

Special Agent Gault set down a small bag of equipment, opened the top and pulled out blue plastic gloves. With his dark-framed glasses and intense look, he fit the classic description of a nerd. Already totally focused on his job, he barely even glanced Livy's way.

"First things first, Ms. Chatham," Pruitt continued. "Did you see anyone when you drove up, or anything unusual?"

Livy looked around. "No. This area is the employee complex and most of my fellow rangers are all still at work. I'm on special duties so I'm…" She hesitated. "I guess you know that. I didn't see anything until I reached the door and saw it was ajar."

"Just ajar?"

She bobbed her head, glad that she was getting her feet beneath her again. "You'll see the lock isn't broken."

Pruitt studied her. "Any idea what they were looking for?"

Livy made a small sound. "That's the million-dollar question, isn't it? What do I have that anyone would be so desperate to find?"

The ISB agent frowned. "Well, we might be able to give you some answers by the time we're done."

Before Livy could ask him what he meant, Special Agent Gault spoke. "Mind if I get started, chief?"

Pruitt nodded. "Go ahead, but I doubt you'll find anything. It seems we're dealing with professionals."

This time Gault looked Livy's way, almost as if he was asking for approval to invade her home. Thankful for the small gesture, she gave him a half smile and a nod. Right now, that little token of respect meant a great deal to her.

Gault paused at the door and began to brush it with powder. Torres turned on a flashlight and entered the cabin behind him. Livy tensed as the stream of light flashed across her living room window, giving her a quick glimpse of a tilted and shredded sofa cushion. She shivered in reaction.

"Livy, why don't you sit in my car where it's warm?"

Ranger Armstead's suggestion was just what she needed. As she followed him to his car, she forced herself not to look back at Hayden. All day long he'd been kind and so conscientious. Now it seemed like he was afraid to get close to her. And maybe that was the problem. Maybe Livy had leaned on him too much, expected more than he was willing to give. It wouldn't be the first time a man had run in the opposite direction when he found out just how needy she was. She'd lost several friends and boyfriends for that exact reason. That's when she'd learned to lean on the Lord, to depend only on Him.

Livy slid into Armstead's car. It was warm. As he closed the door, she heaved a sigh and closed her eyes. She'd slipped up again. Expected a mere mortal to fill the gaps in her life where God was meant to be.

Growing up there were holes in Livy's development, spaces her mother would have filled if not for her illness. Livy spent many of her teen years looking for someone to fit into those spaces before she realized that only God could heal the past and make her feel whole. She thought she'd learned that lesson but apparently she was going to slip up a lot more before she relied on God alone.

She couldn't be hurt or blame Hayden for her mistakes. The only thing she could do was stand up, dust herself off and ask God to forgive her...again.

She prayed, asking for forgiveness, for courage, for strength, and when she ran out of words, she recited her favorite Bible verses over and over again. She must have sat for almost an hour before she finally opened her eyes. It was dark and many of her coworkers had returned home and were now gathered a safe distance behind the vehicles, watching the investigators' progress.

Gault was still working inside her house, but Torres had returned and was exchanging words with Pruitt, Ranger Armstead and Hayden. Her boss nodded and stepped aside to make a phone call. Pruitt gestured for her to join them.

Taking a deep breath, she opened the door and slid out. Pruitt nodded when she walked up. "Feeling better?"

"Yes, thank you."

She ducked her head, avoiding Hayden's gaze. But she needn't have worried. He didn't spare her glance and focused on Pruitt.

The ISB special agent gestured toward her cabin. "So far Gault has found no prints except some which all match and are probably yours. But you're right. Whoever broke in did a good job of tearing up the place. Do you own a computer, Ms. Chatham?"

She shook her head. "No. Not since my old one died in college. I do most everything on my phone."

"Good. Since we couldn't find one, we thought it might have been taken—but now we can remove that from our potential missing items list." He glanced back at the growing crowd. "Come on. Let's go inside where we'll have a little more privacy."

He led the way for everyone and flipped on the living room lights. The switch was covered in black powder. Livy tried not to notice the substance on various surfaces. It only added to the sense of dismal destruction. Torres picked several pillows off the floor and placed them on the couch to sit on. The batting in the sofa's cushions was strewn over the floor.

Livy eased down, trying to suppress her rising unease. The sheer scale of the damage was overwhelming. She didn't own any of the furniture. This cabin came fully furnished by the park but still, the sheer destruction was hard to look at.

Even Hayden, who had been silent since the others arrived, shook his head and a dark frown creased his brow.

Ranger Armstead sighed heavily. "Don't worry, Livy. The park will take care of this. All you need to do is remove your personal items. We'll handle the rest. In the meantime, I've booked a suite for you at the lodge."

Pruitt nodded. "Until we have a better idea of what's going on, I'd prefer you to be surrounded by people we trust. So, for the next few days, Torres will stay with you at the lodge. During the day, you'll be working with Bryant."

"I'm not so sure that's a good idea."

Hayden's comment surprised Livy. She turned a narrowed gaze on him. She understood she had unrealistic expectations of him personally, ones he obviously had no desire to fulfill. But she thought she'd proven her ability to perform her duties and work well with him even under stress.

"You don't want Livy working with you?" The surprise in her boss's voice reassured Livy slightly. At least he still had confidence in her abilities.

"I'm not sure it's safe for her to work with me, especially tomorrow. We're scheduled to leave for the back-country on a day hike at 8 a.m."

Pruitt considered his statement for a moment before shrugging. "I'm assuming this is a group hike and the radio will connect you to base, correct?"

At Ranger Armstead's nod the ISB officer shrugged. "I see no reason to restrict Ranger Chatham's activities."

Hayden's lips thinned into a tight line. "There is a problem. One participant is a close friend of Boyd Goldberg."

That again. Livy almost said the words out loud. Hayden's concerns sounded ridiculous in the face of the wanton destruction surrounding them. What possible connection could a celebrity like Goldberg have to men as violent as the ones who wrecked her cabin?

Ranger Armstead shook his head in a frustrated movement. "I think those concerns are a bit far-fetched, Hayden."

"Maybe not as far-fetched as they sound." Pruitt's quietly spoken words had an impact. Everyone in the room turned to face him. "Let's step this back a bit and start at the beginning."

He leaned his elbows on his knees and clasped his hands together. "One reason we were a bit late arriving on the scene is because we were meeting with the FBI. They had pertinent information concerning Andrew Miller. It seems Mr. Miller had contacted them with information about his employer, Lyra Enterprises. Anyone recognize the name?"

"I do." Hayden's words rang with conviction. "They're an international hotel conglomerate with sites in the Alps and the Himalayas, everywhere climbers congregate."

"Exactly. Apparently, Lyra's very interested in a resort near Hetch Hetchy."

Ranger Armstead groaned. Hayden rolled his eyes and looked away.

"I see you understand the issues." Pruitt spoke in low tones.

"I don't," Livy interjected. "The mountains around Hetch Hetchy are very popular with climbers. Building a resort outside the reservoir on public land sounds like a good idea."

"It was," Pruitt agreed. "Lyra started the project almost three years ago. They even appointed a famous climber to run their climbing program as a way to entice climbers to sign up for the resort's facilities. He's done a good job."

"That program director is Boyd Goldberg." Hayden's tone was filled with disgust. He met Livy's gaze from across the room. It was an "I told you so" look if she'd ever seen one.

Ranger Armstead shook his head. Frustration edged his tense movement. "Just because Goldberg's become the face of a climbing consortium doesn't make him a criminal."

"It does if he's resorting to illegal activities to complete the project," Pruitt added. "Lyra bought up all the public lands outside the park. Some people suggested underhanded activities took place to ensure those sales, including a rather suspicious accidental death of a real estate agent. Blankenship used his authority to get all of that swept under the carpet."

Armstead made a quiet exclamation. "Blankenship is in Lyra's pocket, probably in exchange for campaign contributions. I knew I didn't trust him."

Pruitt held up his hands in a slowing motion. "Actually, Garanetti seems to be the one calling the shots, not Blankenship."

The ISB investigator looked at Hayden. "In fact, it appears Boyd and Garanetti are working together. We haven't been able to verify Garanetti's true identity. But if he is who we believe, he has a rap sheet that goes way back. That's the information Miller was supposed to provide the FBI as well as proof of blackmail and extortion activities connected to the sale of Hetch Hetchy land. Miller said he was being watched. We think he traveled with Goldberg to Yosemite for his El Capitan climb as a cover but Miller died before he could turn his info over."

"Or he was killed before that could happen," Hayden said in a low voice. Everyone turned toward him.

"That fire could have been started to cover up Miller's murder and make it look like an accident. But Livy was a witness to the events and it appears they don't intend to leave any witnesses behind."

Pruitt nodded. "That's a distinct possibility, especially now that Garanetti has disappeared. His room is cleaned out. Blankenship claims he hasn't seen him since yesterday morning and the good representative hightailed it back to Sacramento for what he called 'important meetings.' But I suspect he left quickly to put distance between himself and this situation. If we can find those files Miller was supposed to deliver, we might find the proof we need to connect all the dots."

Ranger Armstead shook his head. "We searched Miller's room after his death and packed all his things into boxes for his nearest relatives to retrieve. There were no files, computers, thumb drives or anything like that. Apparently Miller hid them."

Livy's breath caught in her throat. "They think Mr. Miller told *me* where they were hidden before he died."

Pruitt nodded but Livy's boss protested. "Livy has repeatedly stated that he didn't tell her anything."

Hayden gestured around the room. "Apparently they don't believe her."

He turned to Pruitt. "Do you think it was Garanetti that followed us?"

Livy shook her head. "I'm 90 percent sure it was Dennis Ludlow I saw driving that car."

Pruitt frowned. "I agree. That incident might have nothing to do with Lyra Enterprises. It sounds like something personal between Livy and Ludlow. Frankly, it sounds a little dangerous."

"Exactly. Now you understand why I think it's not safe for Livy to go on the hike." Hayden seemed adamant.

Livy couldn't understand his objections. "If the personal motivation of these criminals poses a problem, then *you* shouldn't be going on the trip either, much less as the leader. From what you say, Goldberg has a grudge against you."

Hayden's features darkened. Normally, she would have been cowed by that black look. But she was determined not to back down. He had every right not to want a closer relationship between them. But he had no right to interfere with her ability to do her job.

Before Hayden could respond, Pruitt held up his hands in a calming motion. "There's something neither of you are taking into consideration. This is an ongoing investigation. The FBI is quietly looking into Miller's background. That's to be expected after his accidental death. So, Lyra and associates might not suspect how deep our involvement goes. That's our only advantage right now. They'll limit their strikes to avoid drawing too much attention to themselves, but only if we allow them to think they're successfully flying under the radar. If you change your routines, they'll know we're on to them and they'll close ranks, stopping our investigation in its tracks. For the time being, our best tactic is to proceed as if these incidents are separate and unrelated. So tomorrow, you will both go on the hike."

Hayden started to protest but Pruitt raised his hands again. "However, Torres will be a last-minute addition to the group. She's an experienced hiker and knows how to climb. She'll be keeping an eye out for both of you. By the time you return tomorrow afternoon, we should have more information and a good idea of where to go from here."

Livy dropped her bag on the floor of the hotel room. It was a small suite. Nice enough, with two beds and a small sitting area, but she wasn't really in the right frame of mind to appreciate it. She was exhausted mentally and physically. All she wanted was a hot shower and to go to sleep.

Maggie Torres dropped her bag beside Livy's. "Do you care which bed?"

Livy shook her head. "The closest one. I feel like I could fall into it now, but I'm headed for the shower."

"Good idea. I'll order us some food."

"I'm not hungry but you go ahead."

Livy grabbed her things and hurried through the shower, eager to relax. She didn't even bother drying her hair. But when she came back into the room, Maggie was sitting cross-legged on her bed with a plate in her hands. On the small sitting room table was a smorgasbord of comfort food options. Pancakes. Mac and cheese. Cinnamon rolls. French fries. A pot of hot chocolate and a pitcher of milk.

Livy giggled. She couldn't help herself. "Do you think you ordered enough food?"

Maggie popped a french fry in her mouth. "Hey, I've been on enough of these incidents to know, the best antidote is comfort food. It's a good thing my boss understands it, too. He never balks at my food bill. Pick your poison."

Livy still wasn't hungry, but a cup of cocoa sounded perfect. She filled a thick mug and curled up on the bed.

"Exactly how many of these 'incidents' have you been on?"

Maggie paused for a moment. "More than I like to think about. Most of the time, I'm doing guard duty like this."

She smiled at Livy before popping another fry in. "I like it. I get to meet interesting people like you."

Livy made a scoffing sound. "I'm not interesting."

"Yes, you are. Ranger Armstead sings your praises, and your record speaks for itself. I certainly didn't save a man's life my second year as a ranger."

"You were a ranger before joining the Investigative Services Branch?"

"Sure. I put in time at the Coronado National Memorial, Death Valley, even the Grand Canyon. I was a ranger for about seven years before I applied for the ISB."

Livy hadn't really looked too closely at the ISB agent. She'd been a little overwhelmed and had only noticed her freckles. But now she studied her. She was shorter than Livy with a curvy figure, a stronger-looking body. She was probably a good climber. Her hair had been in a tight bun at the back of her head earlier but now it was loose, hanging down around her face and reaching almost to her waist. It was the prettiest color of strawberry blonde Livy had ever seen.

Maggie paused in her eating. "What?"

Livy shook her head. "I was just trying to picture you in a ranger's flat hat."

She wrinkled her freckled nose. "Yeah, me and that particular piece of a ranger's uniform didn't get along."

Livy laughed. "Tell me someone who does."

"You," Maggie replied without hesitation. "You could model every piece of the ranger uniform and still look like you belong on a recruitment poster. In fact, you could be any kind of model."

Embarrassed, Livy dropped her gaze. "Why did you make the change to the ISB?"

"My dad says I always wanted to be a policewoman." Maggie shrugged. "I guess he was right. It just seemed a natural transition."

"You must have had some pretty interesting experiences."

"Some but so far, this one has me puzzled."

"How so?"

"Well, I don't get this thing about Hetch Hetchy. I mean, I'm a climber. I like a good cliff. But what makes this place such a focal point?"

Livy sipped her hot cocoa. The mac and cheese smelled good, so she rose and grabbed a plate from the table. Once she was settled again, she lifted one shoulder. "I've only been there a few times myself, but I think I might have some idea. You know how Yosemite forms a narrow valley with the granite cliffs on each side?"

Maggie nodded.

"Hetch Hetchy is like that. Only the valley is filled with water from the dam. There's no boating or swimming on the reservoir. It's one of the purest water sources in the country and the people in charge want to keep it that way. Especially the population of San Francisco, which uses that reservoir as a water source. There's a limited number of hiking trails and not much camping so it doesn't get as many visitors as Yosemite Valley. The area is pristine, and the cliff walls are spectacular for climbing. Visitors from all over the world come to Hetch Hetchy just to test those walls. It's just not as well-known to the average hiker."

Maggie nodded. "I get that having a climbing school

just outside the park would be a good idea, but it seems like there's too much fighting going on to make it worthwhile."

"Not really. The fighting is mainly between the ideological and political factions not climbers themselves. Many years ago, the National Park System did a study to determine what would happen if the reservoir was drained. They discovered that it would only take fifty years for the area to return to its natural state and we would have another national park as beautiful as Yosemite."

"Would that be a bad thing?"

"Some people think so, yes. First of all, if the reservoir was drained, San Francisco would have to find another source of water and they'd have to pay millions for new filtration systems since Hetch Hetchy's water is so pure. Of course, the city is opposed and has been fighting the efforts with an army of lawyers."

She popped a forkful of macaroni and cheese in her mouth. "On the other side of the coin, an army of environmentalists would like to see it drained and the land returned to its natural state. But others fear Hetch Hetchy would become as busy and commercialized as Yosemite Valley so there's disagreement even among them. But no matter what side eventually wins, a climbing school outside the boundaries would thrive."

"So, for the Lyra Corporation it's a win-win situation."

"And for Boyd Goldberg. As a teacher and investor, he'd be set for life. He'd never have to make another death-defying climb, and he'd continue to be a big name in climbing circles."

"Yeah, I've heard all about the rivalry between him and Hayden. That explains the intensity Mr. Tall Dark and Frowning has over this situation."

Livy gave a slow shake of her head. "Hayden doesn't see it as a rivalry, at least not on his part. He gave that life up after the accident that cost him his best friend and his career."

Livy paused. "I think it's more that he fears the lengths Goldberg will go to get what he wants."

"Well, then, there's only one other explanation for the sparks I saw flying between you two. He's got feelings for you."

Livy laughed. "He's got feelings for me, all right, but they aren't the good kind."

"Come on. I saw the way he was looking at you."

"All I am to Hayden is another rescue. He made that point very clear to me just before you arrived." She sent Maggie an embarrassed glance. "I have a tendency to drive men away."

"You're kidding right? Have you looked at yourself in the mirror lately? 'Tall, blue-eyed and beautiful' doesn't usually drive men away. It attracts them."

Livy ducked her head. "Trust me, Hayden's feelings for me aren't like that."

Maggie climbed to the edge of the bed and dropped her legs over the side. "Listen, kiddo, I'm older and therefore wiser than you and what I saw on that man's face wasn't a 'leave me alone' look. It was the 'I'd like to gobble you up' kind. He might have a bit of the 'do I or don't I' blues, but he's attracted to you, for sure."

Livy giggled again. "Do you always talk in phrases like that?"

Maggie smiled. "Always. It's my mother's fault. She had an endless supply of old sayings and silly expressions. They run like a recording through my head. But regardless, I'm not wrong about Hayden Bryant. I'll prove it tomorrow when I get to watch you two up close."

Livy pushed the lone macaroni elbow left on her plate around with her fork. Was Maggie right? Did Hayden have feelings for her? Or was he just in his overprotective search-and-rescue mode?

Maggie was correct about one thing: Livy would know for sure tomorrow. First thing in the morning, she was going to have a talk with Hayden.

The next morning the early sun spilled into the valley from the east, lighting Half Dome and the pinnacle of El Capitan with a golden glow. The air was brisk, perfect for an October hike. Hayden rubbed his hands together, warming them. He'd been in the parking lot trailhead for over an hour. He'd come early so he'd have everything prepared before Livy arrived. He wanted a chance to talk to her.

He knew he'd hurt her feelings yesterday. It was hard to miss the pain that swept over her delicate features when he first arrived at her cabin and held her at arm's length. But it was best this way, better to nip any special feelings in the bud and put distance between them before they developed into something Hayden had no intention of allowing to happen. Livy was a nice girl, too nice and almost girlish in her naivete. Most certainly not his type.

Even as the thought occurred to him, he could almost

hear a little voice asking, *Who is your type...sultry, ma-nipulative Paulette, who you could never really trust?*

Hayden sighed. Livy had questioned his trust in his former fiancée. Despite her off-balance condition at the time, she'd still pegged his situation perfectly...to Hayden's slight embarrassment. And later, when he tried to point out how her connection to Miller made it dangerous for her to take the hike, she'd turned the tables on him and pointed how his connection to Boyd made him equally dangerous to the whole party. Despite her innocent-seeming attitudes, she was no push-over. She didn't have his cynicism, but she did have a keen insight into people.

And she was right. If Pruitt hadn't insisted they stick to their routines, Hayden would have pulled out of the hike today. In fact, as soon as Pruitt would allow it, he would take a leave of absence and step out of the pic-ture. No way would he take the risk of endangering anyone else.

He carried enough guilt.

He needed to explain that to Livy so that she didn't feel...responsible...accountable. He didn't know what to call it. He just knew he wanted her to understand.

Livy and Maggie pulled up in Livy's Jeep. Maggie was dressed appropriately for the hike with climbing shorts and a backpack. He was thankful for that. He'd had little time to evaluate the ISB agent's preparedness for the hike, and it bothered him to have to take her at her word that she was up to the challenge. At least she had all the right equipment and looked fully competent. And what was more, she and Livy were laughing. Their casual attitude made his concerns seem foolish. He con-

sidered not bringing his dark thoughts into their somewhat pleasant mood. But he and Livy had to work as a
team today, so he needed to clear the air between them.

They walked up and Livy surveyed the gear stacked
outside his truck, ready to go. "Wow, you must have
come really early to be so ready."

"I did. I wanted time to talk to you." He glanced
Maggie's way. "Do you mind if we have a private
word?"

She looked at Livy, who gave her a quick nod. "No
problem. I'll just stand over by the trailhead and wait
like any normal participant."

After she'd gone, he turned to Livy, but she held up a
hand. "You don't need to say anything, Hayden. I know
I acted weird yesterday, like there was something between us other than you doing your job. It's my mistake
and I'm sorry. I tend to come across as needy, but you
don't have to worry. I'm back on track now."

Flummoxed, Hayden could only stare. "Well…that
isn't exactly how I expected this to go, but thanks… I
think." He paused as he tried to mentally catch up with
her fast transitions. "I wouldn't have called you needy."

"Oh yes, I definitely am." She nodded firmly. "I've
had plenty of people tell me that I come across as needy
or desperate. You aren't the first man to run the other
way."

"Whoa…" He held his hands to slow her down.
"That's not what I wanted to say."

She tried to smile, as if he wouldn't notice how
strained it looked. "You don't have to say anything.
I know it's true. And honestly, I'm all right now. The

shock of…everything threw me off track, but I spent a lot of time in prayer and I'm okay now."

He shook his head. "You prayed and everything is, okay? Someone started a brush fire that could have killed you, chased you up a mountain and tore up your home but you said a prayer and you're fine."

Frowning lightly, she studied his features. "You don't believe in the power of prayer?"

This conversation was not going in the direction he wanted, and he didn't know how to get it back on track.

"I don't know…maybe…no." He folded his arms. "All right, I admit it—I don't believe saying a few silent words solves a situation or lessens the danger."

She nodded slowly. "I guess that's the difference between you and me. I'm not ignoring it. I just know I can handle anything with Jesus by my side. He's my best friend. I forgot that for a little while yesterday but I'm surer than ever today."

Frustrated, he cocked his head. "Great. Fine. If you're good, I guess I'm good."

She placed her hand on his folded arms. It was tiny, and delicate looking with no marks or scars. He didn't know how she could climb and have hands that didn't show more of the work. His were calloused, scarred and tough as nails. But hers looked slender and delicate. He wanted to reach out and touch them.

"It will be all right, Hayden. I promise. God's got this."

Frustrated and flummoxed, he didn't respond.

But apparently, she didn't need him to respond. She smiled—more sincerely this time—and walked away. Hayden turned slightly to watch her. He hoped she was right and God was in control because Hayden certainly was not. Things seemed completely off-kilter.

The unsettled feeling grew even more when Ron pulled up in his car. Hayden had done everything he could to discourage the disturbing man from attending the hike. Apparently, his efforts had been as useless as his talk with Livy and now he had one more thing to worry about.

Turning his back on the growing group, he surveyed the supplies…maybe for the fourth time. He couldn't afford to be too careful, and he needed the simple, mindless task to help him calm down. The ropes were neatly rolled in circles of eight. He had a pack of emergency supplies and extra batteries for his radio. Individuals handled their own equipment, lunch, snacks for the trail and water. Everything was prepared and was as neat and orderly as he could make it. He consulted his watch. Eight on the dot. Time to move.

He turned to face them. "Good morning, everyone."

The small group of seven attendees, eight now with Maggie, gathered in front of him. He gave them the same safety lecture he'd given yesterday afternoon and asked them if they were rested and confident about today's hike. He resisted the itch to stare at Ron. Conscious of keeping the man's suspicions on the down-low, he didn't even look his way. But as the group broke into pairs, he made sure he was with the troublemaker. He didn't trust Ron with anyone else.

Based on his observations in the class yesterday, he divided them into working duos. Good thing Maggie made their numbers even so he could put her with Livy and know she was safe. A married couple, Linda and Troy Johnston, were naturally together and would do well. Linda had been climbing longer than her husband but Troy made up for his inexperience with greater physical strength. Hayden paired the two remaining, weaker climbers, with two stronger ones. Very experienced Jason Hemmings would be a great match for Sandy Withers, and Chris Lords would be a good partner for Bob Rogers. With everyone smiling, ready and excited, Hayden had no choice but to lead the way up the trail.

The air was still cool, but perfect for the hike up the Mist Trail. The name came from the trail's proximity to both Vernal and Nevada Falls and the mist that settled over the trail from the two waterfalls. It was only about a mile to the first wooden bridge that crossed over the frothy white Merced River. After that, they would ascend the trail at a steep rate. He set a quick pace since they had a four-hour hike to their location. They could make the return at a slower pace.

They walked steadily until they reached the bridge. The water rushed beneath them. Even at this time of year with the winter snowpack long since melted in the summer heat, this part of the river traveled speedily down the incline and was filled with rapids and white water.

They continued to hike at a steady pace, not slowing until they reached the steep steps covered in the mist from Vernal Fall. Hayden did slow down here, not only to take the slick, rocky steps of the trail at a more cautious pace but also to allow the hikers to walk to the lookout to take pictures of the waterfall.

The thunderous waters filled the air with the cooling mist that gave this trail its name. It settled over everything, making the vegetation around the area a dark green. The roar of the falling water drowned out all conversation, but small talk wasn't needed. In Hayden's opinion, the view from the vista point was spectacular and better taken in silently.

A short while later, Hayden headed back to the trail and the group followed. The next leg of the hike was the steepest and the hardest part. Hayden was eager to put it behind them. They reached the top of the falls after a grueling two and a half hours. The class, including Ron, made the ascent to the top in record time. They stopped long enough to admire the view and take pictures, then they were off again.

The trail continued to climb but at a lesser pitch moving away from the cliffs above the valley. This part of the hike was not quite as difficult. The Merced River rushed past them, tumbling over itself, and still casting a spray. As they continued, the river grew deceptively quiet and smooth. They came to the Emerald Pool, a small, shallow lake named so because algae at the bottom gave it a deep green color.

Above the pool was the Silver Apron, a long, smooth slide of granite that swept into the pool. When the water was flowing strong in the spring and summer, visitors often slid down the Silver Apron into the Emerald Pool—illegally. Signs were posted everywhere warning visitors not to enter the water. The current was strong and footing difficult, making an accident far too likely. Many a visitor underestimated the river's power here and ended up going over the falls, a fact Hayden knew too well as the search and rescue lead.

After a while the trail moved away from the river, and peace settled over the group. The clean mountain air, the sparkling sunshine and the deep silence of the forest beside them eased some of Hayden's tension. He began to relax.

Ron seemed subdued. Hayden had no clue what had changed the man from his behavior the previous day, and after a while, he decided that he didn't care. If Ron kept to himself, Hayden might relax even more. In fact, this was a competent group and if not for his concerns, Hayden would have liked the trip to last a little longer.

At last, the trail came to an area that opened into a meadow covered in purple lupines and late summer wildflowers. Opposite the meadow was the base of the cliff they intended to scale.

Hayden halted the group. "Lunch first. Then we'll tackle that little hill."

Everyone laughed because "that little hill" was at least one hundred feet up. But the footholds were solid and manageable, making it a good intermediate climb. He eased off his pack and ate his sandwich. Maggie and Livy sat close by, and he listened to their companionable conversation, punctuated with occasional laughter. They seemed to get along well. Even so, he caught Maggie studying members of the group with a piercing gaze. Her watchfulness gave him another measure of peace.

While he ate, he was gratified to see most of the group, even Ron, examining the cliff, carefully plotting out their path.

Soon the group were packing up their lunch trash and pulling out their climbing gear. He looked at Ron, who was attaching his chalk bag to his waist. "We'll be the last to go. I need to make sure everyone is in good shape before we begin to climb."

Ron nodded. He didn't seem displeased, and he didn't argue, making Hayden wonder again what had happened to the bullheaded man he'd chastised yesterday.

Everyone got off to a good start, climbing strong and steady. Since Ron had been so patient, Hayden let him set their course up the cliff. He chose a good path. The wall had been climbed many times so hooks were already set. As he moved up, Ron did a great job of checking them, hanging on the hooks to make sure they were secure and testing the locking carabiners before releasing the ropes.

Climbing, searching for a good hold and placing his feet in the right spot took all of Hayden's concentration. He was about fifty feet behind Ron when he set his carabiner, braced his feet against the rock wall and leaned back to survey the group. Maggie and Livy were beside them, making good time up with Livy leading. Her slender form scaled the side of the mountain as gracefully as a gazelle…and she was smiling. The effort and the hard work seemed to give her pleasure.

Hayden understood that. He felt the same way—or at least, he used to feel that way before the accident. Now he spent more time overthinking than enjoying. Watching her, he was almost jealous. Turning his focus back on the cliff, he chalked his sweaty hands and hurried to close the gap between him and Ron.

Everyone finally reached the top. The exhausted crew sprawled out on the rocky buttress, panting, laughing and congratulating each other as they rested. At long last, Troy rose to look to the north and enjoy the spectacular view that spread over hundreds of miles, far into the backcountry. Hayden had surveyed the scene many times. It was an amazing sight. That view was the main reason he chose this particular cliff to climb. Suddenly, Troy froze and turned to him, his features wrinkled with concern.

Hayden stood, his eyes catching on the same thing Troy had seen. Smoke filled the northern skyline.

The backcountry fire was fifty or more miles away, but their spectacular location afforded them a bird's-eye view of the growing conflagration. Flames covered the horizon, as tall as the pine trees they were torching. All the distant skyline burned. As they watched, the center point of the flames began to circle round and round. Eventually a slender spike of fire twisted and crawled into the sky, circling as it climbed.

"What's that?" Sandy Withers's tone echoed the fear that was growing in the pit of Hayden's stomach. "Is that what I think it is?"

The finger curved and turned. It moved in slow motion and looked unreal, like a cartoon or a movie CGI but it was very, very real. Slowly but surely, it twisted into a pillar of fire shooting high into the atmosphere.

"That, folks, is a firestorm." Hayden tried to keep his voice calm. "A fire so large, it creates its own weather system, complete with wind currents."

Sandy turned terror-filled eyes in his direction. "You mean it's a fire tornado?"

Hayden silently nodded.

Livy stepped up beside him. "All the smaller fires must have joined to make this a complex."

Hayden agreed then took a slow, deep breath. "All right, everyone, the fire is still far away. But I think it's best we save time and not climb. We'll take the trail behind the mountain to get back down. Pull up your ropes and let's head back."

The group began to move, gathering gear and packs. Hayden worked, too, winding his ropes. He kept his movements controlled and easy, like he wasn't in a rush to get away. He even tried to make a joke about how they should have practiced a fire drill yesterday.

But no one smiled or laughed. Not even Hayden. Everyone knew how unpredictable a fire could be. Urgency underscored their movements. In spite of Hayden's confident assurance that the fire was far away, they all felt the need to put as much distance between them and the raging inferno as possible.

FIVE

Livy watched Hayden as he led the party back down the trail. She and Maggie were at the back of the group, making sure there were no stragglers. But that wasn't really necessary. Everyone was hurrying. In fact, Hayden stopped the group twice to force them to slow their pace, cautioning them to be careful.

"We don't need an injury on the way down. Let's just keep a steady, normal pace and we'll get back in plenty of time."

The hiker who did the worst job of regulating his pace was Ron. Now that they'd discovered the proximity of the complex fire, he seemed agitated almost beyond control. Livy wasn't sure what had happened to the belligerent man she'd encountered the day before, but she'd been relieved he'd calmed down for the better part of the day. It had been pleasant until they discovered the fire. Now Ron was overly concerned and nervous. Something had happened to him. He was acting like he was being chased…by something more than a fire in the distance. He was following Hayden so closely, he was almost on his heels. At one point, he stumbled and fell forward right into him. Thankfully, Hayden managed to catch them both and keep them upright.

Gripping Ron's arms, Hayden looked him straight in the eyes. "You need to calm down, Ron. The fire is still far away. We'll be fine. Just take it easy."

Ron's head bobbed vigorously. "Yes, yes, of course. Thanks. I will."

Livy shook her head in confusion. His current behavior was a far cry from the man who'd confronted her yesterday. What could have possibly changed him so much?

Beside her, Maggie spoke in low tones. "That guy is on the edge. Why is it always the big ones who cave at the first sign of danger?"

Livy nodded in agreement. He was definitely on the edge, but she didn't think the fire was the real reason. It seemed he was expecting something…more.

She watched Hayden reassure Ron quietly again, then pat him on the back in a friendly, buddy-like way. After that Hayden led them down the path with a purposeful stride.

Watching Hayden, Livy bit her lips in silent regret. Hayden was the perfect leader. Strong. Courteous but authoritative when needed. He was the best climber she'd ever seen. He was also a kind and honorable man, and handsome on top of that. In short, he was everything Livy ever could have wanted in a partner…except for one thing. His words from earlier this morning echoed over and over in her head. He didn't believe in prayer. He might not even believe in God's existence.

As much as Hayden appealed to her, as much as she yearned for his occasional smiles and strong companionship, they could never be together. Livy could never yoke herself to an unbeliever. His dark and doubting nature would destroy her own hard-earned faith and peace. It would drag her into a hole from which she might never recover. She couldn't allow that. She needed a partner whose faith could pull her from the brink when she slid to the edge. Hayden wasn't that person no matter how strong and capable he was in other areas.

It pained her to admit it. She cared for him more than any other man she'd ever met. But they could never be together.

The disappointment she felt proved that what she thought was just a crush was actually something more, something deeper. These few days with his concerned companionship wrapped around her had been wonderful.

It was going to take all of Livy's strong religious conviction to keep her from giving more of her heart to a man who didn't want it—and wouldn't know what to do with it if he got it. No matter how much she might desire and wish it could be Hayden beside her, it simply couldn't be. Wishing and wanting more would only make parting more difficult.

Confirmed in her resolution once more, she took her gaze off his striking form leading the way and focused on the small, worried group of hikers behind him.

Despite Hayden's warnings, the party trekked along at an almost too brisk pace. The trail narrowed as it entered the canyon cut out by the Merced River. They were forced to slow down. The air was cooler here and felt better than the blaring heat of the upper portion of the trail. Livy sighed with relief as cool air drifted up from the river. She paused to rest and inhaled deeply.

Was that smoke? She looked around, wondering if the complex fire had come closer. Or maybe the wind had shifted, bringing the smokey waves down the river canyon. But the scent passed, and she turned her focus back to the narrow trail.

The path dropped more, almost to the level of the river's edge. Usually, this shady place just off the river was a good spot to rest and cool down. But today, Hayden didn't pause. Instead, he motioned Ron ahead of him. He stepped to the side of the trail to speak to the hikers as they passed.

But suddenly Ron stopped and froze, his gaze fixed on whatever he saw around the bend. The rest of the group bunched up, crowding the narrow trail at his back. Maggie and Livy hurried forward to see what had stopped them all in their tracks.

Around the bend, flames licked the trees on top of the next rise. The small fire was just a mile away and it blocked the trail. Hayden pulled his radio from his pack.

"I knew it. I just knew it!" Ron's voice shivered with anguish and he stepped back, off the trail.

"What do you mean? What did you know?" Maggie's voice was tense.

"I suspected they were up to something but they played me. Used me to get you. They were lying about everything!"

Hayden put the radio down and held up one hand. "Calm down, Ron. I'll call in the report and find out what's going on."

"I can tell you what's going on. They planned it! I

overheard them talking and they saw me. Now they're out to get me, too."

Dread built inside Livy. "Who is out to get you, Ron?"

"Boyd and his cousin! I heard them on the phone talking about a fire. When I asked Boyd about it, he said they were discussing the blaze in Tuolumne last week. He convinced me that everything was all right and I should go on the hike. I should have trusted my instincts. There had to be another reason Boyd was suddenly treating me like his best friend. He's the one who told me to take this class."

Ron turned to Hayden. "He said you were a good teacher and then he made a joke. He said those that can't do…teach."

The man looked up. "He hates you. Wants you gone." He shook his head and backed up. "And now I know too much. He's out to kill me, too."

"Kill? What makes you think he's trying to kill Hayden?" Maggie's agent instincts seemed to kick into high gear.

Ron shook his head. "We have to get out of here. We have to go before they kill us all." Panicked, his gaze shot around. "We have to cross the river and get away from the fire."

He stepped back again, closer to the water.

Hayden yelled, "Stop, Ron. We can't cross here. The current is too swift. We can't take the chance. We'll find another way around the fire."

The panicked man shook his head. "No…no, we have to get away. They won't stop. They won't ever stop!"

Ron took two more steps back. His foot slid off a

moss-covered rock, and he floundered, his arms waving madly in the air as his backpack pulled him backward. Maggie, Hayden and Livy lunged forward, but they weren't quick enough. He splashed into the water. In an instant, the swift current caught him and carried him downstream.

Maggie started into the water, and Hayden put out an arm to stop her. "I don't need you going down, too."

He looked around. In less than a heartbeat, he spun and climbed up the hill. He slid his pack off his shoulders, dropped the radio on top and unhooked his rope. Livy did the same. She knew what he was planning. Maggie quickly followed suit.

They needed to get downriver, in hopes of catching Ron before he struck a rock or was pulled under.

As Hayden ran around the bend in the trail, he shouted back. "The rest of you stay here…and stay out of the water!"

Livy ran as fast as she could. She was just behind Hayden when he lunged to the left, off the trail. The trail went into a switchback as the river curved around another rocky promontory. Hayden was taking a shortcut, over the ridge, hoping to get ahead of Ron in the swiftly moving water.

Livy didn't hesitate to follow him up the hill and over the rise. Their path was thick with overgrowth. A small pine branch Hayden had pushed out of the way swung back and struck her in the face. She gritted her teeth and kept going, but she soon found that Hayden was moving at such a brisk pace she couldn't keep up. She had to slow down.

When she finally broke clear of the underbrush, she

saw they had emerged on top of the ridge. The trail was about five feet below her. She jumped down and barely managed to land solidly. She heard Maggie do the same but she landed with a small gasp of pain. Livy turned back.

Maggie was bent over, grasping her ankle. Livy hurried toward her, but Maggie motioned her on. "Go on! Help Hayden. I'll be right behind you."

Livy nodded and spun. She leaped sideways down the gravelly hill to the river's edge. She could see Ron downriver. His pack was stuck on a log jammed against a rock. His head was bowed, as if he was unconscious and his mouth was dangerously close to the water. Only the pack, caught on the log, was keeping him afloat. One good bump and he would go under.

Hayden had already unwound one end of his rope. He looped it around his waist and tied a knot.

As Livy came up, he motioned to the rope still coiled on the ground. "Wind the other end around that pine twice and secure it with a knot."

He headed to the water before he paused and looked back. "Whatever happens, Livy, don't come in after us. If I can't get Ron out, don't risk your life, too. Get the rest of those people to safety any way you can. I couldn't live with myself if I lost more people on my watch."

Livy nodded her head slowly, but he didn't wait for an answer. He'd already started to wade into the water.

The current immediately caught him and swept him down toward Ron. The current was too fast. It was going to carry him beyond the man's location. Hayden stroked with his powerful arms. He made headway, but it wasn't enough. The current carried him just below Ron.

Suddenly, Hayden's head went under water. Livy cried out and started toward the water.

"Stop, Livy! He told you not to go in."

Unnoticed, Maggie had come up behind her. She was limping but able to walk.

Livy shook her head. "We can't just stand here and watch them both drown! We…"

At that moment, Hayden's head bobbed back out of the water. Livy let out a sigh of relief and muttered a quiet prayer of thanks. He hadn't hit an underwater rock or boulder as Livy feared. In fact, he had a hold of Ron's leg. Hayden must have lunged underwater to grab it. He let the rope secure him as he latched on to Ron's leg and pulled him loose from the rock. Then with the big man cradled in his arms, Hayden leaned back and let the current carry them both downriver until the rope securing them was taut.

He would not be able to pull them both back without help. Livy slipped off the button-up blouse she wore over her tank top, wrapped it around the rope and started to pull them in. It took a few minutes for Maggie to hobble over to the rope, but she tugged, too.

After a few minutes, it was clear they weren't making headway so Livy stopped. "Hold on. We've got to work in tandem, not at the same time. You pull and then I'll pull. That'll give us time to rest in between."

"Got it." Maggie grasped the rope and pulled. As she did so, she kept the rope close to her body. Livy grabbed it with her shirt-wrapped hands and picked up where Maggie stopped. They worked together for ten minutes.

The men were coming closer to shore, but it was slow going. Hayden was attempting to help by pulling with one arm. The other was latched around Ron, who seemed to be coming to. But they were still too far away for Livy's comfort and she could tell that Maggie's strength was fading fast. Planting her feet, and pushing against her injured ankle was taking its toll. Livy didn't know how much longer she could pull on her own and they had a long way to go to bring the men to the shore. The current was simply too strong.

Suddenly, Bob, Chris and Jason appeared in front of Livy and grabbed the rope.

"We'll take it from here."

All three men pulled, heaving and muscling the heavy load. Maggie dropped to the ground in exhaustion. Livy bent over, trying to rest her arms. Relief made her weak. If the men hadn't shown up, she didn't know how long she and Maggie could have kept it up.

Thankfully, the three men working together were able to bring Hayden and Ron to the water's edge. Livy ran to them. Grasping Hayden under his arms, she pulled him the rest of the way on shore. He never let go of Ron and both men were too heavy for Livy. She fell to her bottom and dragged them over her legs. It felt like it took the last of her strength—but it was enough. Both men were on solid ground. Even then, Hayden had a hard time releasing Ron. It wasn't until Chris and Jason lifted Ron fully out of the water that Hayden let his arms fall.

Livy lay on the ground behind him. After a long while, she pushed him upward. His shoulders were cold to the touch and the muscles in them were tight from exertion. "You did it."

Hayden shook his head and gave her a slight smile. "*We* did it."

Jason came to his side. "Come on. Let's get your feet out of the water."

Hayden laughed as Jason helped him rise. "That's fine with me."

They found a sunny spot for Hayden to rest and warm up, but only for a moment. Smoke from the new fire was already drifting their way.

While they waited, Chris examined Ron's head. He was conscious but slightly groggy. Still, he reached for Hayden's hand and shook it. "You saved my life. I'm sorry I put you in so much danger. I felt betrayed and used. It terrified me, and…"

"It's all right, Ron. Boyd has a way of doing that."

Livy felt the need to apologize, too. Hayden had warned her from the beginning that his climbing rival was a dangerous man, and she hadn't believed him. But she would have to wait for a later time to have that conversation, maybe when they were alone.

Chris fingered the bump on Ron's head and he winced.

Hayden looked up. "You look like you know what you're doing, Chris."

"I'm just an inhalation therapist but I know the basics. I think he might have a slight concussion. I don't see any of the serious signs they tell us to look for. The most important thing is to make sure he doesn't go into shock."

Hayden nodded. "Right. We need to get him warm."

Livy watched him shiver. "What about you?"

"I'll be fine. I have my climbing shoes in my pack and another shirt. My lightweight pants will dry soon enough."

Livy motioned to her wet shoes and pant legs and Ron's pack sitting on the edge of the bank. "Me, too. But Ron's spare clothes are in his backpack and are soaked."

"We'll figure out something. Let's get back to the group."

Chris and Bob helped Ron to his feet. Hooking his arms over their shoulders, they half carried him up the riverbank to the trail. Jason looped Maggie's arm over his shoulder, and they made their way up. Hayden and Livy climbed the bank together, but all the way back, Hayden's words echoed in her mind.

I couldn't live with myself if I lost more people on my watch.

The small group stayed on the trail rather than hiking over the bend to reach the rest of the group. Hayden and Livy trailed behind. It gave him time to take stock of the group. Moving was slow going even with Chris and Bob helping Ron. Halfway back, Ron seemed to recover somewhat and his movements became steady. But Maggie grew weaker with every step. Even with Jason's help she had to stop more and more frequently. Finally, Livy stepped up, took Maggie's other arm, and looped it over her shoulder. With both Livy and Jason working together, they were able to brace Maggie enough to keep going, and they finally arrived at the spot where they'd left the others.

The Johnstons and Sandy seemed more than relieved to see them. Sandy was visibly agitated. When they came around the bend, she stopped her nervous pacing back and forth in midstride.

"At last! We thought we lost you, too!"

Hayden recognized the near panic in her voice. He needed to present as calm a facade as he could manage. "We're fine. We just need a minute."

Even after the exertion of walking back, he and Ron were still chilled. The river water came from the high Sierras and carried the cold of winter snow with it. They both needed rest. Most of all, Hayden needed time to think. But time wasn't on their side. He needed to make some decisions as fast as possible.

He took his spare clothes out of his pack and went up the path to change behind some bushes. As he stripped off the cold, wet clothes, he reviewed their situation. Given the proximity of the brush fire on the trail, they were going to have to move back up the mountain to a space suitable for a rescue helicopter to land...if there was one available. All the federal and Cal Fire units were already trying to contain the complex fire, and now, the park rangers would be busy evacuating visitors below the trail.

Hayden heaved a shivery sigh. Their situation wasn't desperate, but it certainly wasn't great. He needed to keep everyone calm and safe until they could figure out an evacuation route. Rolling his wet clothes into a ball, he headed back to join the others.

Ron's clothes in his pack were soaked, so the group scavenged through their own things to find something warm and dry for him. Livy had already pulled the first aid kit out of Hayden's pack.

Not for the first time, he was glad she was his partner in this venture. As much as he hated to see her in danger, he was glad she was working with him. She was the best kind of ranger to have in a crisis...she wasn't a bad one to have in easy times either. A picture of her scaling the cliff so effortlessly flashed through his mind. But he pushed those thoughts away.

His mind was wandering in dangerous directions. He must be feeling the aftershocks of his plunge in the river. Ron was clearly feeling them, too, sitting on a rock and shivering in spite of the silver solar blanket from the first aid kit that Livy had given him. They needed to do more for him.

Hayden nodded. "Right. We've got to get to a place where we can make camp and light a fire."

"A fire? Don't we have enough of those?" Sandy's tone still echoed with panic. That reaction was the one Hayden wanted to avoid. He met the frightened woman's gaze and glanced pointedly at Ron. Her lips tightened into a thin line of frustration, but she nodded and said no more.

"Once we find a place on the trail with an open space and get settled, I'll radio headquarters and find out what's going on. For now, let's get moving."

Giving the group something to do was the best antidote Hayden knew to keep the fear from taking hold. No one argued. They gathered their packs and started back up the trail. Livy and Jason half carried Maggie. Chris and Bob stayed by Ron's side. He seemed in control and alert but mentioned that he had a lingering headache from the bump on his head. They couldn't go far or fast. He needed rest.

Hayden tried to picture the trail ahead, to think of a good place to stop. But he still felt slightly disjointed. Despite his best efforts just to move forward, Ron's words lingered in his mind.

Boyd was out to get him. Not just Livy, but him, too. And who was Boyd's cousin? Had they really started the fire on the trail?

He forced those thoughts out of his mind. Whatever the situation was with Boyd, there was nothing he could do about it at this time. Right now, his first concern had to be the people in his care, mainly the injured ones—Maggie and Ron.

They trudged silently back up the trail, putting a good mile between them and the fire. The path dipped down toward the river and widened into a spot backed by a ten-foot rocky ledge. It was a perfect place to build a fire and to take stock. He called a halt. Maggie eased down on a rock with a sigh. Ron plopped down on a large, slanted boulder. It was warm from the sun, and he stretched out on it, soaking in the heat.

Chris threw another dry shirt over the big man's legs. Bob glanced at Hayden. "I'll gather some wood for a fire."

"Good. I've got a lighter in my pack." Thankfully, he carried supplies for all occasions.

Livy came to him and held out her hand. "Give me your wet clothes. I'll spread them out on one of those rocks beside Ron's. Maybe we can get them dry before the sun goes down."

He did as she bid and when he handed them to her, he grasped her fingers in gratitude for one long moment. Had it only been seven hours since he looked at her hand on his arm and wished he could touch it?

He clung to them for a minute. Long enough to feel their grip. They may have looked dainty but they were strong, just like she was. An unexpected wash of warmth swept through him.

"Thanks for listening to me back at the river. I didn't need one more person putting themselves in danger."

She paused. "I didn't stay out of the water because you told me to. I did it because it was the smart thing to do."

"It *was* the smart thing to do."

She started to turn away but spun back. "You do realize that it was teamwork that got you and Ron out safely, right?"

Frowning, he nodded. "Of course. Why would you ask?"

"Because of what you said about not losing one more person. You may be the search and rescue lead, but I'm a ranger. These people are my responsibility, too."

"I never doubted that."

She nodded slowly. "Just so we're clear. I know I haven't been at my best the last few days but that doesn't mean I can't do what I've been trained to do. We're a team. I don't need you shouldering my share of the burden."

"I didn't mean it that way."

Squaring off to face him, she met his gaze. "Then exactly what did you mean?"

Shrugging, he looked in the distance. It had been a spur-of-the-moment comment stemming from the idea that he couldn't bear to lose one more person he cared about. That realization shook him more than he wanted to admit, especially to Livy.

He ducked his head. "Let it go, Livy. It was a tense situation—I barely even remember saying it. You're a great ranger. There isn't anyone I'd rather have working beside me than you."

Surprise washed through her features. Her guarded stance loosened, and a smile spread over her lips. "Thanks. I just thought—well, after what happened last night at my cabin, I thought you didn't have confidence in my ability to do my job. It's good to hear you do."

That unexpected, sunny smile warmed him almost as much as his dry clothes. For the first time, he was glad for her perpetually positive attitude. He needed that extra shot in the arm right now.

At that moment, Bob returned with some dried grass and small sticks to start the fire. "This is enough to get you started. I'll go look for some bigger stuff."

"Thanks." Trying not to show the reaction Livy's smile created in him, he stooped and built the sticks into a small pyramid.

"I'm going to go talk to Sandy," Livy announced. "Maybe I can reassure her."

If anyone can do it, it's you.

Hayden didn't say the words out loud. He simply nodded and kept his gaze on the work at hand. But Livy's special kind of happy glow stayed with him as she walked away. He focused on surrounding the pile of sticks with larger rocks. By the time Bob returned, the small blaze was large enough to handle the bigger pieces of wood he'd found.

He turned the maintenance of the fire over to Bob and went to check on Maggie. "How are you holding up?"

Maggie motioned to the river behind her. "I think if I put my foot in the cold water, it might bring the swelling down. After that, I'll wrap an ace bandage around it. If someone could find me a branch sturdy enough to serve as a walking stick, I'll be ready for the next leg of our journey."

Jason had been standing nearby, and now he stepped up. "I'll help you down to the water, Maggie."

The young man had been hovering around the ISB agent even before the accident. Smiling to himself, Hayden decided he could count on Jason to look after her.

"Just don't get too far into the water. I don't want to fish anyone else out."

Maggie gave him a firm shake of her head. "Don't worry about that. I saw enough to never trust that current, no matter how gentle it looks."

Hayden stepped back and surveyed the group. Once again Livy was right. Teamwork was going to get them through…even him. Small doses of Little Miss Sunshine were also helping.

Everyone had something to occupy them for a few minutes. Nodding to himself, he took the radio from his pack and headed away from the group. He heard something behind him and looked back to see Livy following. He didn't stop her. In fact, he appreciated the backup.

He found a spot some distance away and clicked the call button on the radio. As soon as he did, multiple calls came over. The rangers were speaking back and forth, working on evacuating visitors on the valley floor.

"This is Hayden Bryant, over. Can anyone hear me?"

"We hear you, Hayden, go ahead."

"I'm on the Mist Trail with Ranger Chatham and a class of eight students, ten people total. We were returning from a hike into the backcountry when we encountered a brush fire. Is the trail blocked?"

"Affirmative, Hayden. Firefighters are on the scene. They've prevented the fire from traveling down into the valley, but their efforts have pushed the fire in your direction. We are aware of your situation and have been working with the air force to bring in additional helicopters for an evacuation."

"We need that evac as soon as possible. We have two injured members. One man with a slight concussion and Maggie Torres has an injured ankle."

"That's new information. We were hoping you could make it back up the mountain to a different location. Will confer and get back to you."

"Roger that. I'll await new instructions."

He turned to Livy but from her expression, she understood what they meant. They would not be evacuated before morning.

She gave him a brisk nod. "I'll go take stock of our supplies and see if we have enough to get through the night."

"Just check the food. I have a water filter in my pack, so we can get more from the river. That will have to do."

He glanced back at the group gathered around the small campfire. "My main concern is Ron."

Livy nodded. "I'll take Chris aside and see if he has an update on his condition."

"Hurry back. I want to give headquarters a detailed picture of our status."

He watched Livy move around the group, gathering supplies and calming concerns. She really was a top-notch ranger. Just the kind you needed in a situation like this. Why hadn't he recognized that about her before?

The answer was simple. He was too busy looking for reasons not to like her. He'd been attracted to her from their first meeting. His own stubborn refusal to let anyone get close made him search for a way to keep his feelings locked inside, with Livy outside.

Closing his eyes, he turned his back on the group. Right now, with danger so close, he didn't know if the realization of how much he liked her was a good or bad thing. If they didn't make it through this—if something happened to Livy—he'd find himself fighting loss again. He wasn't sure he had the strength or the courage to face that once more.

With his back turned, he didn't see Livy return. "The Johnstons have a large bag of trail mix they're willing to share. Everyone has energy bars, and you have a big bag of beef jerky in your backpack. That will give everyone a little shot of protein to hold off the hunger. We should have enough to keep us okay until morning."

She'd just finished speaking when the radio squawked, and Dale came on. "Glad to hear from you, Hayden. We were worried. How is your group?"

"We have one man with a possible concussion but he's not showing any signs of immediate danger. Maggie injured her ankle trying to help us pull him out of the water. I'd prefer to get them back and have them checked out right away, but it sounds like that won't happen."

"There's not enough daylight to send a helicopter out...even if we had one to spare. In addition, that complex fire has created some vicious air currents hampering our efforts. The air force assured us they will send us two of their smaller aircraft at first light. Can your group make it to the meadow below the cliff?"

Hayden glanced at Livy. "That puts us close to the complex fire, Dale."

"I know. If you have a better idea of a place to land a helicopter, I'm all ears."

Hayden shook his head. "You know there's not a better option."

"Right. So, get your group to a good location to camp for the night then head out in the morning for the rendezvous."

"We're about two miles below the meadow."

"Roger that. I'll have the air force helicopter in flight at the crack of dawn. You just keep your people safe until then."

"I'll do my best, Dale."

"Switch the radio to another channel where we can talk more privately. I'm afraid there's more bad news."

Hayden did as he was told and clicked on to a private channel. "How much worse can it get?"

"Well, for starters, we found the car and identified the driver that trailed you the other day."

"You found fingerprints in the car?"

"No. We found blood. Apparently, the ride down the mountainside was more difficult than you thought. The driver's head hit the steering wheel, and he bled quite a lot. It was a good thing we had his blood on file."

"It was Dennis Ludlow," Livy murmured before Dale could continue. "He cut himself on a box cutter at the store and had to have stitches at the camp clinic. It got infected and he had to have additional treatments."

Hayden nodded before he clicked the radio on. "So have you found Dennis yet?"

"We haven't found him and now Boyd's disappeared along with his cousin."

Hayden met Livy's gaze. Her lips were parted in that surprised, wide-eyed gaze he found so captivating.

She released a breath and murmured, "Of course. *Dennis* is Boyd's cousin."

Hayden nodded back as a piece of the puzzle clicked into place.

He clicked the radio on. "It all makes sense now. Dennis has been working behind the scenes for Boyd all along. That's why he was willing to settle for a job in concessions when what he really wanted to do was fight fires."

Dale's firm voice echoed over the radio. "Roger that."

Shaking his head, Hayden clicked on again. "Boyd was supposed to make his climb today. Did the fire cancel it?"

"He didn't make the climb but the fire wasn't the reason. He disappeared last night. The FBI had gained some information and were looking for him for questioning, but he was gone. They interviewed workers at the Lyra facility in Hetch Hetchy. It seems Garanetti was known around the facility as the Fixer. He took care of problems and cleaned up messes. In fact, he's also wanted for questioning in connection with those suspicious circumstances surrounding the death of that real estate agent in Hetch Hetchy."

"I was right. Another 'accident' like Miller's death?"

"Exactly. We put out an APB for Garanetti, and Dennis Ludlow for their obvious connections. We also put one out for Boyd as a person of interest. So far all three men have completely fallen off our radar."

"The FBI is convinced Boyd is involved?"

"Definitely. Representative Blankenship said he hired Garanetti on Boyd's recommendation. So we're pretty sure he's involved, but we can't prove anything without Miller's files. Pruitt thinks Garanetti is eliminating any chance of the authorities finding them."

"Any chance…meaning Livy."

Dale didn't answer but he didn't need to. Cold washed over Hayden, and he stared at her. She looked as shocked as he felt.

He shook his head. "Finding the files won't help Boyd. He was already losing his sponsorships. This record climb was designed to bolster his falling credibility. If he missed it, his career will be seriously damaged."

Dale agreed. "At this point, he's a desperate man. I think it's safer up there for Livy with a fire between her and those men."

Livy closed her eyes and turned away. Hayden punched the button on the radio. "Don't feel so confident, Dale. Ron, the hiker I warned you about? He panicked and jumped in the river because he overheard Boyd talking to Dennis about a fire. Ron is convinced Boyd and his cousin started the fire on the trail to trap us. That could mean they're up here with us."

The radio was silent for a long while. At last Dale clicked on and his voice sounded troubled. "Do you think he's right?"

"I'm certain that *he* believes it. He was scared enough to try to cross the Merced even though I warned him not to. We just got him out. That's how he was injured."

The radio was silent for even longer. When Dale came back on, his voice was heavy. "Post a guard tonight, Hayden. Keep a watch on everyone. I'll have the air force helicopters in the air at first light. I want you back here as soon as possible."

"Roger. We'll do our best to keep everyone out of harm's way."

"I know I can count on you and Livy. You are some of the best I have."

"Thanks, Dale. I'm going to shut the radio down to conserve the batteries. I already need to put in my spares. I want to make sure I have power tomorrow for the rendezvous. But I'll check in at nine tonight and at five in the morning to make sure our plans are on track. Signing out."

Hayden clicked off the radio and pushed down the antenna. Livy walked away to stare at the dark billowing smoke from the distant complex fire. Her shoulders were stooped, almost as if she was in physical pain. He could imagine what she was thinking...the same thing he would be in her shoes. How far would the danger and damage to the park go just because she tried to rescue a dying man? How many more people would lose their lives?

He walked up beside her to stare at the columns of smoke. "This isn't your fault, Livy. You didn't cause this."

She didn't look at him. Instead, she shook her shoulders loose, as if she was shaking a weight off. Then she turned. "It will be all right. God is good all the time."

Hayden stood for a moment longer, resisting the urge to hug her. He was so glad her thoughts were not traveling down the same path as his. Where he saw nothing but cause for despair, Livy found the hope and strength she needed to go on—and in the process, she shared it with him. It was a rare gift.

He wanted to tell her so but not expecting or needing a response from him, she turned and headed back to the group.

SIX

Hayden explained to the group that they'd be spending the night on the mountain. Livy thought they took it well. They probably expected it after all that had happened. As Hayden went over the details, he didn't repeat Ron's words that someone had started the fire to trap Livy. For that she was thankful. All she wanted right now was to get everyone off the mountain safely. Not that she couldn't take criticism, but blaming her or anyone else wouldn't make their efforts any easier.

Sandy and Linda helped her filter water from the river and fill everyone's water bottles. The Johnstons' willingness to share their trail mix was a blessing, as well as Hayden's package of beef jerky. They divided some extra energy bars and passed them around. That made up their evening meal. It wasn't really filling but helped abate the hunger pains.

Now everyone had bedded down around the fire. Ron's clothing had dried on the rocks but not his backpack. It was still wet, so he rested his head on Livy's pack and was soundly sleeping while she took the first watch.

Maggie had soaked her ankle one last time in the

cold river water before propping it on a rock and lying down. Jason lay close to her, within arm's reach. Hayden was stretched out close to Livy, sound asleep, exhausted after his efforts in the river. That's why when he said they needed a lookout, she volunteered. She knew he needed rest to be his best in the morning.

She watched the firelight play over his features. While the others had pulled out sweaters or windbreakers, Hayden's only covering was his knitted cap, pulled down low over his ears. His dark beard shadowed his cheeks and strong jaw. His long lashes rested on his cheeks. Even in sleep he was handsome.

Livy forced herself to look away. She gazed up at the sky. To the north, smoke clouds shadowed the stars. To the south sparse, smokey clouds filtered across the moon. She thought maybe the firefighters were winning the battle with the brush fire on the trail. At least she hoped so.

Directly above her, the stars twinkled in the midnight sky. In ordinary circumstances, without the fires, the sky would have been brilliant, the stars and planets seeming so close, it seemed as if she could almost reach out and touch them. It would have been a beautiful time, here by the fire with friends nearby, tired but triumphant with a long day of climbing behind them.

What would it be like to spend the day with Hayden, just the two of them? To share a campfire and talk about life? She felt like he had so much to share if she could get past the wall he'd built around himself. He could tell her what it had been like to be an international star with adoring fans. How it felt to save so many lives here in the park, and how he went on after the tragedy that had struck him. That was the main question she wanted to ask him. How he let go of the ones he lost.

She couldn't stop seeing Mr. Miller's body sprawled out on the cliff edge. Every time the image came to her, she prayed for the man and for herself. It seemed to help. But Hayden didn't pray, and she wondered how he managed to go on without it.

Suddenly, he jerked and made a small sound. He was having a nightmare. Fearful he might wake the others, she reached across the space and placed her hand on his chest to give him a little shake.

"It's all right, Hayden. We're safe."

To her surprise, he came instantly awake. Frowning, he rose and wiped a hand down his face.

"I'm sorry, I didn't mean to wake you, but you were having a nightmare."

He nodded and pulled his cap farther down over his ears. "It happens frequently since the accident."

She inhaled lightly. "Do you want to talk about it?"

He gave an immediate shake of his head. "No, I want to forget it."

Shrugging, she picked up a stick and stirred the fire. "You might as well go back to sleep. It's a long time until my shift ends."

Crossing his legs, he tucked his feet underneath him and shoved his hands toward the fire. "I won't go back to sleep for a while. Once the dream wakes me, it takes a long time to settle down."

She bit down on her lips so she wouldn't ask again if he wanted to talk. If ever there was someone who needed to, it was Hayden Bryant, but she refused to be annoying and ask one more time.

He heaved a sigh. "I'm not going to discuss it, but you might as well say what's on your mind."

She gave him a slight smile. "Am I that obvious?"

"You couldn't be clearer if you spelled the words out on your face."

She nodded and shrugged. "It's not about the dream exactly, but I've been sitting here all night, thinking about Andrew Miller."

She stirred the fire again. Embers crackled and flew in the air. "I can't stop seeing him on that ledge, reaching for me."

Her voice cracked and she looked up at the night sky. "I know what happened to him is not my fault and I did all I could to save him. I just can't stop seeing him on that ledge and I wondered…" She hesitated. "You've made so many rescues… I just don't know how you stop seeing them."

Hayden placed his elbows on his bent knees and leaned forward. The firelight flashed over his face and lit a golden glow in his brown eyes. He didn't speak for a long while, but when he did, his voice was low.

"I don't see them all. Just the really bad ones." He ducked his head. "The children are the worst. I don't ever forget those. But most of the rescues I make are of young males between the ages of eighteen and thirty-eight. They get themselves into trouble because of ego and bravado. They think they can beat the odds, or they overestimate their skills. And then they wind up hurt and trapped in difficult places. I look at them like a situation to be handled…sort of like a cliff that needs climbing. I just concentrate on the challenge, like I used to do when climbing. That way I don't see the person, just the job that needs to be done. At least not until it's all over. Then all I want to do is lecture them for being stupid."

Livy chuckled. "I think I witnessed that yesterday when you tore into Ron."

He smiled and his teeth gleamed white in the dark curls of his beard. "Yeah, I was pretty rough on him. I can't tolerate that kind of careless attitude, not on a climb."

Right then, without him saying another word, she knew what nightmare plagued him night after night. It was the one where his climbing challenge resulted in the death of his friend. And just as suddenly, all the pieces slipped into place.

Hayden kept most of his rescues out of his dreams because he treated them like challenges. They weren't people, because if he let them be real, be human, he'd start to care for them and then he would suffer if they didn't make it. Emotionally, he kept them at arm's distance just like he did everyone else in his life.

It might have been the saddest thing Livy had ever heard, even sadder than her own past. Taking a deep breath, she looked away.

"Well, if you're going to stay awake, I think I'll lie down."

He shrugged and tossed her his backpack to use as a pillow. "Sleep well."

Livy nodded and eased down on the pack. It smelled just like Hayden, like pine trees and musk. Closing her eyes, she released a slow, sad sigh. It was going to be a long time before she actually fell asleep.

It seemed only a few moments had passed when she woke to an exclamation.

"Fire!"

She came awake slowly. Her weary mind tumbled over her thoughts. Hayden had spoken but his word didn't make sense. The fire shouldn't have come this close so soon.

"Wake up, everybody! We need to get moving."

She rose slowly, blinking her eyes. Behind the ridge, back the way they had come, flames lit the sky. That jolted her into alertness. She leaped to her feet and looked around. Hayden stooped to grab his backpack and slide the straps over his shoulders.

Chris ran back from the bend on the trail, straight toward Hayden. "It's a fire all right…and it's close. We have to get out of here."

Livy shook her head. "The fire was almost out when I went to sleep."

Hayden met her gaze, his dark eyes once more lit by the flames of the campfire. "It's a new one. I spotted it and asked Chris to check it out."

Livy's lips parted in surprise as his words registered. A new fire. Started by someone following them, driving them toward the complex fire like rats in a lab maze. It had to be Garanetti, Boyd and Dennis.

Panic set in and, for half a minute, Livy froze, not moving.

Hayden grabbed her shoulder. "It's only about a half a mile away. We have to go."

His low spoken but intense words finally galvanized her into action.

"I have one flashlight. Does anyone else have one?" Hayden held his up and looked around.

No one answered.

"Then we'll have to use some torches from the fire. Chris…"

"I've got Ron."

Jason hefted his backpack on his back. "I'll help Maggie."

Hayden looked at Livy. "Can you see that every trio gets a small torch?"

She nodded. "And I'll make sure the fire's out when I leave."

He hesitated for a moment, almost as if he wanted to say something to her. But he simply nodded before spinning and leading the way up the trail with his flashlight. Chris and Ron followed.

Jason handed Maggie her makeshift walking stick, and she hobbled up with his help. Livy pulled smaller branches from the pile of wood they'd gathered and held the ends in the fire. She handed the first one to Jason.

Sandy slid her pack in place. "I don't need one. I'll stick with the Johnstons." Livy handed a torch to Troy and the threesome started out.

Bob grabbed plastic bags from his pack and hurried to the river. While Livy lit another stick, he filled the bags with water and carried them back. They stirred the embers. Bob poured one last bag full of water onto the flames and Livy gave it a final stir. Then they took to the trail, far behind the rest of the group.

Bob carried the burning stick. The trail climbed out of the culvert they'd rested in. Ahead of them, she could see the next group's lights, climbing the trail, staggered far apart. It made her nervous that they were all spread out and even worse, carrying torches with them, but it was the only way to see along the dark and twisting trail. Once they reached the top, she would feel much better.

She and Bob set a brisk pace and soon caught up with the Johnstons and Sandy.

Troy had a hold of his wife's arm. "Exhaustion and the smoke from sleeping near the fire has triggered her asthma. She needs to take a puff from her inhaler."

"I'm all right. Really."

Livy touched her back. "It's all right, Linda. Better to stop now while we can."

As the woman looked through her pack for the small inhaler, her husband gave Livy a silent nod of thanks. She smiled at him then glanced back at the fire. It wasn't growing fast, but it was climbing along a line, almost as if it was tracking the trail. Fires didn't burn like that… unless they were being helped along with an accelerant.

She was almost certain someone was back there, triggering and directing the fire. But fire had a mind of its own. In this dry season, it could spread out of control in a heartbeat. Whoever was back there was in as much danger as they were hoping to create for Livy and her party. She wished they would realize that. With his background, she was sure Dennis knew that. But he'd already shown that he didn't care about his own safety when he went over the edge of the mountain in the white vehicle. Apparently, whoever was with him didn't care about their personal safety either.

Bob came back to where she was standing. "Ron was right. Someone started this fire, didn't they? That's the only way it would burn along a line like that." He kept his voice low so the others wouldn't hear.

Livy nodded. "Yes, I think so, but let's not mention

it to everyone else. We don't want them panicking like Ron did. We need our group to concentrate on getting to the landing spot. Why don't you take the lead?"

He agreed and headed up to the front of the line, encouraging the others as he moved. "Let's go, folks. We need to put some miles behind us."

They followed without comment, but Livy stayed behind to watch the fire. After a few moments, she turned and caught up.

The next portion of the trail was narrow, and they needed to stay close together to see. Bob hurried ahead, climbed on a rock and held the torch up high for the others to cross beneath him.

Thankfully, the puff of medicine seemed to help Linda's breathing, and they made good time uphill. They caught up with Maggie and Jason, who were having trouble walking side by side on the narrow trail. Bob took Jason's torch and put it out. Then he led the way up with his torch, leaving Jason with both hands free to assist Maggie.

It was still slow going, but no one complained. Livy said a silent prayer of thanks for the good people surrounding her. It was a wonderful reminder that God was good all the time, even in troubled times like these.

The last stretch of the trail was the steepest and the narrowest. Livy stayed behind as the group climbed. Bob stood on the rock in the center again, holding the torch high so everyone could see.

Troy stepped in front of Maggie. "Hold on to my waist and step with me. That way, Jason can hold you from behind. Use me as your walking stick. Only step when I step. That will help you keep your balance."

Maggie nodded, in too much pain to speak. Livy took her walking stick and held it for her as the trio stutter-stepped their way up the narrow trail, accommodating Maggie's limp. Troy's idea worked well enough but Livy held her breath until they were over the top and disappeared.

Bob hopped down from his perch on the rock. "Our turn. Let's get out of here."

She followed him up the incline. As they came to the crest, she paused one more time to look back. The fire had crept over the ridge. Fiery branches fell onto the area where they had camped and sparks flew through the air, swirling around in the culvert.

Her gaze followed along the ridgeline. For one fleeting moment, she saw movement. Then as one large pine tree exploded in flames, she glimpsed three figures running away from the fire. They disappeared into the trees.

"Are you sure?" Hayden asked, then waited for Livy's response.

"I'm sure. I couldn't make out features or anything distinguishing, but I know I saw three figures running away."

Everything inside him tensed, and he studied his ragtag group. Ron was still suffering from a headache but had kept up. Maggie was worse off. Exhausted and in pain, she lay back against a rock with a hand over her eyes. Hayden didn't know how much farther she could go. But one thing was certain, her climb up this last, steep incline had taken its toll. She needed a good, long rest.

"I'm going to scout the trail ahead, see if I can find something to use as a travois for Maggie. We've got at least another mile and a half of hard hiking and she looks spent. While I'm gone, tell Jason, Bob and Chris I need to meet with them when I get back. I'll need their help."

After a quick look at his watch, Hayden hurried up the trail. It was almost time to check in with Dale on the radio. The eastern sky was turning gray. Soon, the rescue helicopter would take off from its airbase…and they still had a long trek ahead of them. He needed to let Dale know they would be running behind. Building the travois would eat up precious time, but it had to be done. Maggie couldn't make it otherwise.

Here at the crest of the incline, the trail widened, snaking along the lip of a cliff that dropped to the river below. The cliffs on both sides of the river formed another narrow canyon for the river. The sound of rushing water and rapids echoed up to Hayden.

Turning in the opposite direction, he hurried away from the edge of the forest and stepped beneath the deep shadows created by the tall timber. He didn't have to go far before he found two sturdy branches about six feet long. Using their climbing ropes, they could tie the two poles together in a V and stretch his solar blanket between them. It would make a bed for Maggie. The men would have to take turns dragging her along, but they would make better time than her current limping pace could manage. And they needed to make good time. Smoke was already drifting toward them from the complex fire. The scent filled the air, seeping deep into the shadowy pines.

Hayden carried the wooden branches into the open then turned on the radio to contact Dale. At first, all he could raise was static. The complex fire was creating winds that hampered even their radio contacts.

At last, Dale came on. "Good news. Your transports will take off in half an hour. We're sending two smaller helicopters to accommodate your group. All the larger ones are already in use. Once they lift off, it will take them another hour to reach you. That's an hour and a half span. Can you make it to the meadow by then?"

Hayden breathed a little easier. "I hope so. We're a quarter of the way there already."

"You left before sunrise?"

"We had to. Fire reached us along the trail."

"That's impossible. We have the brush fire trail completely contained."

"This is a new fire—and it had help getting started. Livy saw three men running into the forest. I think it was Garanetti, Goldberg and Ludlow."

Dale's radio was silent, and Hayden could imagine Dale expelling his frustrated words on the other end before clicking back on. At last, the head ranger opened his channel.

"I understand Garanetti. He's a criminal. He's gotten away with so much in the past, he thinks he can do it again. But why would Goldberg take that chance? He's wanted for questioning but we can't prove anything yet. He should be lying low or trying to leave the country, not chasing you and Livy deep into the mountains."

Hayden shook his head. "If Boyd thought he could get the files and destroy me at the same time, he'd consider that a great solution."

The radio was silent a while longer. "I'm sorry I didn't believe you about Goldberg, Hayden. You were right all along. And I'm even more sorry you're trapped up there. I shouldn't have let you and Livy go on this hike."

"It's not your fault, Dale. Even I never dreamed Boyd would go to these extremes. And when we made the decision, we didn't know about Garanetti's criminal past. It was a calculated risk, and we all agreed to it. Besides, you'll have to get in line behind Livy to take the blame for underestimating Boyd. And neither of you are at fault. I doubt I sounded all that rational when talking about him."

"None of that matters now. All that's truly important is getting all your people and yourselves safely off the mountain. We can form a blame line later."

"Roger that."

"Do you have enough power on your battery to leave your radio on? I want to know your progress."

"If the helicopter is less than two hours away, I've got enough. I'll keep it on."

"Good. Signing off…and, Hayden, be careful. Don't let your guard down for a minute."

Hayden started to respond but Dale had already clicked off. The sudden loss of his authoritative voice sent a momentary spike of fear shooting through Hayden. The sound of the rapids rushing by and the scent of creeping smoke almost unnerved him.

Somewhere out there were three driven men, determined to stop them. Nature's most drastic elements were trying to overwhelm them and nine people were depending on him. It was the stuff of his nightmares.

He took a deep breath and exhaled through pursed lips. At least free climbing wasn't involved. He didn't have that stress. All they had to do was hike up the trail. They could make it. He could push them that far. Hefting the six-foot sticks and tucking them under his arms, he jogged back to the others.

When he arrived, the men of his group were waiting. He explained how to shape the litter for Maggie. Livy had already given one of the extra ropes to Chris for Hayden to cut up and use. They set to work.

They crossed the two pole ends in an X and lashed them together. The opposite ends extended in a V shape. Then they tied ropes crisscrossing the poles and draped the silver solar cover over them. Last, they fashioned a harness for two men to drag the litter along. Hayden was discussing the rotation when Sandy strode toward him.

"Is it true? Are there men following us and starting fires?"

Hayden looked around. Bob ducked his head. "I saw the men and mentioned it to the group."

This wasn't how he'd wanted them to find out, but he wasn't going to lie—and it wouldn't do any good to browbeat Bob for jumping the gun. "It's all right. I was going to tell you all. Yes, we are being followed and yes, we think they are starting the fires. They're trying to force us toward the complex fire."

"Not us," Sandy said, her voice rising. "Ron said they're after Livy. It's her they want."

Livy was silent but her features reflected the pain Sandy's words caused. Hayden needed to squelch the accusations before they went any further.

"Those men aren't just after Livy. They'd like to see me dead, too."

Sandy gasped and shook her head, tears pooling in her stressed gaze. "Why? Why did you two bring us up here? How could you endanger us like that?"

Linda nodded her head in agreement. Her husband looked away, not sure whether to support his wife or defend the others.

To Hayden's surprise, Ron spoke up. "He didn't know! Neither of them knew the danger they were in. If anyone should have stopped this, it should have been me. I could have told Hayden what I knew. But I believed those men's lies. If it's anyone's fault it's mine."

Sandy turned an angry glare on Ron and Linda seemed about to jump in as well when Hayden raised his hands. "Everyone calm down. Just calm down!"

His tone was the one he used on injured climbers when they panicked. It carried command and usually worked. Thankfully, it seemed to have the same effect here.

When they stopped shooting visual daggers at each other, he spoke again. "None of us are to blame. The fault lies with despicable men behind us. Let's not give them any more help by losing our control now."

Sandy took a shaky breath. Troy wrapped a comforting arm around his wife's shoulder. She smiled and nodded at him. Both of them comforted Sandy. She dissolved into tears and fell into Linda's arms.

Hayden inhaled and paused, gathering his own control before speaking again. "The good news is we have two helicopters on their way. We're wasting time arguing when we should be walking to meet them. Troy and

Linda, I need you to lead the way up the trail while the rest of us take turns with the litter."

Troy seemed to straighten up at the invitation to take charge. Grabbing his wife's pack, he helped her slide it over her shoulders. Then he handed Sandy hers before slipping into his own. He looked at Hayden and nodded.

"Go ahead, Troy. Bob and I will take the first shift with Maggie. We'll go as far as we can, then we'll need Chris and Jason to spell us. Everyone ready?"

Even though Hayden felt confident that he'd quelled some of the rising tension in the group, he was still relieved to hear their agreement spoken out loud. Everyone started walking. Jason helped Maggie ease down on the litter. When Chris attempted to help Ron, he shook off his help.

"I can manage. Take care of Maggie. She needs you more."

The big man hefted his backpack and trudged up the trail. Hayden wrapped his spare shirt around the rope halter so it wouldn't rub against his and Bob's hands. They both slid the looped ropes over their heads and settled them around their waists.

Hayden met his partner's gaze. "Ready? On three. One…two…three."

They both stepped forward. The litter lurched and bounced but it moved. It took them several yards to find a rhythm where they were working together. Once they achieved it, Hayden was pleased at how quickly they moved.

A healthy person could hike three miles in an hour. Their speed would be much slower, but they should still arrive at the meadow in plenty of time.

He and Bob pulled for half an hour. When Hayden saw his partner struggling, he called a halt. Maggie needed a rest from the bouncing as well. She lay back on the litter, a hand wrapped over her eyes.

"Any more pain reliever, Chris?" Hayden kept his tone low.

The man shook his head. "I gave her the last of it this morning."

"I'm fine, Hayden. Don't worry about me," Maggie spoke up, but in spite of her brave words, her tone was laced with pain.

She wasn't fine, but he appreciated her brave effort. Jason and Chris picked up the halters and strode forward. Shaking his arms and shoulders, Hayden dropped back.

Livy had been following far behind the group. Her gaze constantly scoured the surrounding area and her features twisted into the pained look she'd first adapted when Sandy slung her accusations.

He moved into step beside her. "Any sign of them?"

"No. Not since I first saw them. The fire blocked the trail so they couldn't follow us that way. They had to work their way through the forest. They're probably far behind us now."

"You're right. So maybe you can stop worrying quite so much."

Her lips thinned into a hard line, and she shook her head. "I'll stop worrying when you do."

He paused. "I'm the lead of search and rescue. Worrying is my job."

She stopped, too, and turned back to face him. "It's my job, too, Hayden. You keep forgetting that I'm a ranger.

This group is also my responsibility, maybe even more than yours and I won't rest until they're all safe on those helicopters."

Gesturing to the men pulling the travois, she continued. "Teamwork is what saved you and Ron in the river, Hayden. Teamwork is going to save us all."

He frowned. "Of course it is."

"Then please stop trying to keep me from doing my job."

He couldn't halt the surprise sweeping through him. "When have I tried to stop you from doing your job?"

"At the river. You told me not to go in after you."

He shook his head. "No one else needed to risk their lives."

"Maybe, but you don't get to decide how I respond, Hayden. I've been trained to assess and make my own decisions and from where I sit, the one person in this group who is not expendable is you. I should have been the one to go in the water after Ron. Not you."

He shook his head. "I couldn't have…" He stopped midsentence.

A sad, sorrowful look came over her features. "Exactly. Your need to be the lone wolf does a pretty good job of keeping people at bay in your personal life, but it has no place here. I'm going to do my job no matter what. We're a team and I'd appreciate you keeping that in mind."

She moved ahead, and he stayed behind, watching her walk away. Bemusement filled him.

Her assessment of his feelings was on target. He still felt he'd made the right choice when he'd gone into the water and ordered her to stay on shore. But she was correct when she said his decision had nothing to do with their jobs and everything to do with his desire for her not to get hurt.

He could barely acknowledge his own motivations, but within days of their close association, she had him pegged.

He shook his head. On top of being a good ranger, Livy was exceptionally wise.

With all he'd learned about her, how had he missed the band of steel running through her slender body? He'd attributed her Goody Two-shoes attitude to na-ivete…a youthful lack of understanding when it came to how tough life could be.

The longer he knew her, the more he realized her positivity came from a will strong enough to overcome every obstacle in her path.

It was a new, complex facet to Livy…one he was ex-tremely glad to have on his side right now.

SEVEN

The sun rose but was obscured by the haze of smoke coming from both fires. Livy stayed far behind the group, constantly searching the forest and trail. The three men pursuing them had to be far behind, but Livy's group had been slowed down by Maggie's litter. Livy had no idea how long it would take the men to catch up, so she stayed vigilant.

She'd been a bit harsh in her conversation with Hayden. If she was honest with herself, most of her anger didn't come from Hayden's treatment of her on a professional level. Most of it was personal. She'd fallen all over herself to apologize to him yesterday morning. She took the blame, assumed she had come on too strong and driven him to put up a wall between them. She had thought his unspoken rejection was personal, but it wasn't. Hayden put up a wall with everyone. He kept them at a distance so he wouldn't care...wouldn't be hurt again if something happened to them.

Last night by the campfire she'd longed to talk to him, to understand how he got past the pain of loss. Now she knew. He didn't let himself get close to anyone. If he never got close, he never had to suffer loss again. He could do his job without the pain of connection.

He had marked a hard, lonely path out for himself and there seemed no way she could cross the barrier he'd erected.

She understood that and accepted there was no future for them—but there was no way she would allow him to put her in imaginary bubble wrap and keep her from doing her job. That nonsense stopped now. Her sense of duty was as strong as his. She had worked hard to survive and just as hard to become a ranger. She wouldn't allow anyone to take that sense of purpose and accomplishment away from her, even someone she was half in love with.

Those thoughts pushed her forward for the next mile. Hayden and his partner did two more turns dragging Maggie's litter. They were moving forward quickly but the day had warmed up and Livy could see the exertion was taking its toll. Also weighing on them was the smoke that filtered through the air, causing some in the party to cough. Even Livy's lungs burned slightly from irritation and exertion.

At last, they turned a bend in the trail and the broad meadow where they ate lunch yesterday appeared. Was it really only yesterday? So much had happened, Livy felt as if days had passed.

She glanced at her watch. They had a half an hour before the helicopters were due to pick them up. Half an hour during which she needed to be extra vigilant.

Troy and Linda dropped their packs in a clear area on the edge of the meadow and sat down. Sandy followed suit. Ron did the same, but Chris and Jason hurried back to help Hayden and Bob pull Maggie the rest of the way. The four men dragged her to a shady spot beneath a grouping of trees.

The ISB agent was obviously suffering. The bumping and jarring had probably caused almost as much pain as her injured ankle. But the group had traveled faster than she could have done on her own. Livy hurried over to give her a sip of water and a handful of trail mix she'd been saving.

Maggie drank the water thirstily, almost emptying the bottle before catching herself.

"Sorry." She wiped her mouth and handed Livy the bottle back. "I didn't mean to drink it all."

Livy shook her head and spoke in a low tone. "They'll have more for us on the helicopter. Drink what you need."

Maggie insisted she take it, so Livy sipped until the bottle was empty. They sat in silence for a while longer.

"I'm sorry this happened to you."

The agent shook her head. "Don't be sorry. This is my job. I'm supposed to be taking care of you, but I messed up. I should have been more careful with my landing."

Livy shook her head. Hayden's words that day in the restaurant kept echoing through her mind. "If I hadn't been so…so busy trying to save the world one fool at a time, maybe none of us would be here."

Maggie gripped her hand. "You didn't force Andrew Miller to create a file and you especially didn't push him off that cliff. But you were there to hold his hand when he died. Don't let bad men's actions destroy the good you've done."

Livy looked around at the ragged, exhausted people scattered through the meadow and shook her head. "Tell me how I helped these folks. If you can find an answer to that, I'd really appreciate it."

"Without you and Hayden we never would have made it out of here."

"Without me, you might not have been in danger at all."

Maggie sighed. "Look, Livy, evil men do evil things. Someone has to stop them. That's why you and I do what we do. From what I've learned about these guys, they would kill anyone who got in their way. I'm just thankful this time it was someone like you and me who make it our job to get in their way."

Livy nodded slowly. After Sandy's accusations, she'd been so busy feeling guilty she hadn't thought of it in Maggie's terms. But she was right.

Gripping the agent's hand, she smiled. "When this is all over, let's do a girls' day at the spa. Just you and me. Manicures and massages. Deal?"

Maggie grabbed her hand. "Absolutely! We'll get the works. We've earned it."

Livy smiled.

Just then, Sandy rose to her feet and shouted, "Listen!"

The group grew quiet as the distant whop of helicopter blades echoed over the clearing. Livy laughed and Maggie squeezed her hands again. They all stood and watched as wisps of smoke parted and one helicopter lowered down through the layer of smokey haze.

One helicopter, not the two they'd been promised. Livy glanced at Hayden, and he gave a small shake of his head. She got the message not to say anything to the others.

As the helo touched ground, he ran forward, ducking beneath the blades. Livy followed him.

An airman hurried to the side of the vehicle and climbed out.

Hayden grabbed his hand in a shake. "Boy, are we glad to see you."

"We're glad we made it. The other helo didn't."

Livy gasped, but no one else heard it over the roar of the blades above them.

The airman shouted over the noise. "The winds from the complex knocked it into some trees. It sustained damage and had to turn back. I don't think another one can make it through. We're not even sure we can get out."

The whooping of the blades echoed above them as shock rolled over Livy. Hayden turned to her, his silent gaze searched her face. She steeled her features, determined not to show him the panic she was feeling.

At last, he turned back to the airman. "How many can you take?"

"Eight—maybe nine, but that would be pushing it. We're not even sure we can lift off with the downdrafts that firestorm is creating."

Hayden nodded slowly. "I'll stay behind. You'll have to make it nine."

Livy shook her head. "Eight. I'm staying, too."

"No way, Livy. You're getting on that helo." Hayden's shout was loud enough to be heard over the noise.

Determination hardened inside her. "Protecting this group is *my job*, Hayden Bryant, and that means giving them the best chance of being able to take off and get out of here. That'll be easier for them with eight instead of nine, and you know it. It's my duty to stay here, and neither you nor those men behind us are going to stop me from doing it."

He studied her face, seeming to take in every minute detail as his eyes swept over her, and settled on her mouth for one intense moment. His gaze was tender. Almost loving.

Shock rolled over Livy. Hayden cared about her, really cared.

Not only did he care, he desired her. She had doubted he had feelings for her, but those doubts ended right there and then. And it gave her one more reason not to abandon him alone, here on the mountain.

Warmth flowed through her as he continued to focus on her lips, but she didn't shift or even blink for fear he might think her resolve was faltering. Even the airman stood poised, motionless as the helicopter blades spun around and the current swept wisps of her hair into the air.

At last Hayden turned to the airman. "I'll need another radio. The battery on mine is almost dead."

The man nodded. "You got it as well as more water and some MRE rations. Anything else you need?"

Hayden leaned in. "Reports on the fires. What's happening with the one behind us?"

"It's moving east, away from the river."

"Good news. Livy and I will climb down to the river and try to make our way back to the valley."

"Keep us posted. If we can get clear of the winds

of the complex fire, we might be able to stage another pickup."

Hayden nodded. "We'll load our two injured hikers first. Livy, get the supplies from him while I get Maggie and Ron."

She followed the airman back to the helo. He handed her three large bottles of water and four packs of MREs. Then he followed her to the group.

Hayden pointed the airman toward Ron and Maggie. "They're our injured members."

Ron had risen to his feet. He took the airman's arm and headed toward the helo. The look on Hayden's face must have telegraphed the change in plans. Turning back, he halted.

He held out his hand to Hayden. "Thank you for… everything."

Hayden grasped and shook it. After a firm nod, Ron allowed the airman to lead him away.

Maggie, however, was in too much pain. She obviously didn't realize something had changed until she looked up and saw the supplies in Livy's arms. "Wait! What's going on?"

"The other helicopter was damaged and had to turn back," Livy explained. "This one can't take all of us, so Hayden and I are going to climb down to the river and make our way back on foot."

"But it's too dangerous! The fire's back there."

Hayden took the supplies from Livy's hands and stuffed them into his pack. "The fire has turned away from the river, Maggie. The two of us can climb down faster than the rest of you and make it to the water's edge. We'll be safer there."

She turned back to Livy. "We can all fit on the helo. We have to."

Livy shook her head. "It'll be too weighed down. With us gone, you all have a better chance. Besides, Hayden will need a partner for the climb down. We're too far above the river."

She gripped her friend's hands. "Get on board, Maggie. The helo needs to get going."

Not hesitating any longer, Jason picked Maggie up and carried her toward the helicopter.

Maggie looked over his shoulder and shouted, "I'm counting on our spa date. Don't you dare let me down!"

Livy smiled and waved as the Johnstons and Sandy followed them. Sandy hesitated and turned back to mouth the words *I'm sorry.*

Livy smiled at the older woman. Sandy returned the smile and hurried away.

Chris grabbed Hayden's arm. "I'll stay, too. I'm a good climber."

Hayden shook his head. "I appreciate the offer. If the helo can't lift off, I'll take you up on it. But right now, climb on board and let's see what happens."

Chris hesitated. It was clear that he wanted to disagree but his common sense won out. Grabbing his pack, he jogged to catch up with the Johnstons and Sandy and helped them climb into the helicopter.

Bob reached for Hayden's hand. "I'll see you back at the valley, boss."

Hayden smiled and shook hands with him. Then Bob followed his fellow hikers. Once they were all inside, the airman stood in the door and waved. The copter's engine revved, louder, and louder. Its whine increased almost to the point of being painful to the ears and still it didn't lift.

Livy held her breath, fearing it wouldn't take off. Finally, the tail lifted slightly. Slowly but surely, it rose into the air. Standing in the open door, the airman gave them one last wave before the helicopter disappeared into the dense smoke.

Smokey wisps whirled in circles where it had been. The sudden silence seemed empty. Lonely.

Livy drew in a long, shuddery breath.

Hayden turned to her, frowning. "You should have been on there."

"No, I shouldn't have been. You saw how difficult it was to take off. I'm right where I need to be."

He lifted his shoulders in a frustrated shrug. "Let's get going. We need to get down to the water where the air will be clearer. I'll contact Dale when we get there."

Lifting his pack, he shoved the radio inside. Livy picked up hers and slid the straps over her shoulders. They both turned and headed back toward the path. A noise behind them made Livy pause. She turned back.

Three men—Garanetti, Boyd and Dennis—marched toward them. Garanetti held a rifle pointed straight at Hayden.

"Hold it right there. You're not going anywhere."

Everything inside Hayden curled into a ball of anger as the men moved forward. From the minute he'd heard Boyd's involvement confirmed, his gut instinct told him Boyd would find a way to get at Hayden.

All three men looked the worse for wear. Their clothes were dirty and torn. Dennis's hands looked like they might be burned and Garanetti had a deep scratch across one cheek. Boyd was the only one with no visible injuries and even he was far from pristine. But no matter how ragged they looked, nothing could mask the hatred blazing out of Boyd's gaze.

"Put your hands up," Garanetti ordered. He held the rifle with confidence, like he'd done it many times before. If he was the man Pruitt thought he was, he had. He was a killer.

Livy raised her hands, but Hayden hesitated. Glancing down the path, he tried to gauge how far they would have to run before they turned the corner on the trail.

Garanetti scoffed. "Don't mistake me for these two fools. You won't get that far."

Boyd turned to glare at the man but said nothing. Obviously, the agreement they'd reached was a shaky one. That mistrust could help Hayden and Livy.

Grim resolve filled him, and he slowly raised his hands. "Maybe, but you are the kind of fools who set fires to trap us and ended up trapping yourselves."

The man smiled, but it wasn't pleasant. "No, we're not trapped. Our transportation out of here should arrive soon."

Hayden resisted the urge to look into the sky. They had to be waiting for a helicopter. Did they know the firestorm winds had reached epic levels?

If Hayden could stall, they might get flustered when their ride failed to arrive. That distraction could create an opportunity for Livy and him to make their escape.

Garanetti gestured to Dennis. "Get their radio."

Dennis hesitated a moment, until the man motioned him forward, pointing the muzzle in his direction. Ducking his head, Dennis crossed the distance between them.

Inhaling sharply, Livy shook her head. "I understand how you hate me, Dennis. But how could you set those fires? I thought you loved this place."

Garanetti didn't allow Dennis to answer. "He doesn't love this place more than his life, which is not worth much now."

Boyd stiffened. "We had a deal. We help you find these two and we go free."

The tall man shook his head. "If Livy doesn't talk, then we'll have to take extreme measures to make sure no one ever finds those files."

His ominous words made Boyd step back. Even Dennis reacted with fear to the man's menacing words. Hurrying across the meadow, Dennis unzipped Hayden's backpack and pulled the radio out. He returned and handed it to Garanetti, who dropped it on the ground then swiftly used the metal stock of the rifle to smash it before flinging it deep into the trees.

He turned to Livy. "Now, tell us what Miller said to you."

Hayden's mind scrambled for something to say. "Don't tell them anything, Livy."

Garanetti tilted his head. "If you don't talk, I'll shoot Bryant."

"He's going to kill us anyway. Don't tell them anything."

Garanetti smiled. "True, but I can make your death very painful. I don't think Livy would like to watch that happen."

Livy tensed. "Miller didn't say anything to me that day."

Garanetti nudged his head toward Dennis. "He says he saw you on the cliff. Miller talked to you."

She glared at Dennis. "He watched us from a mile away with a pair of binoculars. He has no idea what really happened."

Dennis made a low sound and his features twisted. "I saw you speak to him and take his hand. That's more than you ever did for me."

His tone and words were so pathetic, Hayden could almost feel sorry for him. Still, if Ludlow was that emotional over Livy, maybe Hayden could use those feelings to their advantage.

Livy shook her head. "I talked *to him*. He didn't speak to me, Dennis. He couldn't. He was dying."

Could he provoke the man into lashing out? Maybe it would create enough of a distraction for him to be able to get the gun away from Garanetti. With that idea in mind, Hayden spoke up. "It's pretty sad that you're jealous of a man losing his life, Ludlow. Besides, from what I hear, Livy tried to help you, too."

"Shut your mouth, Hayden. My cousin doesn't need help from the likes of you." Boyd's tone was vitriolic.

Hayden smiled. "Sounds to me like both of you need all the help you can get. I hear your climb got canceled, Boyd." He gave his rival his most self-satisfied look just to egg him on.

It worked. Boyd growled and stepped forward. "You're going to—"

Garanetti shouted, "Enough. We're wasting time."

He turned to Livy. "Tell me where Miller hid the documents."

She closed her eyes and her shoulders stooped. "I don't know. He told me nothing. He tried to talk, but he was badly injured, with almost no strength left. He just…chattered. Nothing I could even identify as a word."

Before the man could reply, a squawk came from the radio strapped over his shoulder. He lifted it off and pulled it close to his mouth before speaking into it. The only thing Hayden could catch was the word "where."

Garanetti grew agitated and yelled into the radio. It was obvious that something was wrong. The pilot must be having trouble getting to them. Just then, the sound of a helicopter echoed over the meadow. They all turned. Garanetti spoke another burst of frantic words into the radio but there was no response.

Suddenly, the helo dipped. The landing rails clipped the tops of several tall pines. Branches and pine needles shattered and flew across the meadow. The helo wavered from side to side then dropped to the ground like a rock, landing hard. Dust and dirt flew up around it.

They all ducked from the flying debris. Livy fell to the ground. So did Hayden, mainly because he'd seen a large softball shaped rock at his feet. While the three men exchanged shouts and angry words, Hayden dug the rock out of the ground and cupped it in his hand.

"Stay here. Watch those two," Garanetti shouted at Dennis and handed him the gun before running toward the helicopter.

"I'm going after him!" Boyd spun. "I won't let him go without us!"

He ran after Garanetti. When they were far enough away, Hayden swiftly rose to his feet and threw the rock with his best pitch. It struck Dennis right in the temple. The stone connected with a thud, and he slumped to the ground without a sound. The men didn't notice, focused on the still-whirring blades of the copter as they struck rocks and dirt. Metal screeched and glass shattered.

"Run, Livy, and don't look back." Hayden kept his tone low. She rose in a quick movement and dashed down the trail.

Hayden waited one moment longer, making sure Dennis didn't rise. Boyd and Garanetti didn't turn their way. In fact, they began to shout at each other. A small fire erupted in the grass around the downed helicopter. Boyd dropped to his knees on the ground and began scooping dirt onto the blaze to try to extinguish it, but it was growing fast.

Hayden didn't wait any longer. He spun and followed Livy. She had already reached the bend in the trail. Within minutes they both had turned the corner, out of sight of the meadow. But they didn't slow down. They kept running as fast as possible.

Soon they turned another corner, still with no sign of the men following. But Hayden didn't ease up their pace. The men would surely be following them soon. They were determined and desperate. They wouldn't give up easily. Hayden and Livy needed to put as much distance between them as possible.

He and Livy would be safer by the river. But they had far to go before they would reach an accessible cliff to climb down to the river's edge. For now, they had to keep running.

They were both in good shape but still, in their weary state, they had only gone a half a mile when Livy began to show the strain. She tripped and only avoided falling because Hayden grabbed her by the backpack.

"Come on," he said as he righted her. "Let's slow it down a bit."

She nodded and bent over to rest for a moment.

"We can't stop, Livy. We have to get as far away as possible."

She nodded again, too out of breath to speak. But she rose and stepped out quickly, striding strong and sure.

They had gone another half mile when a massive explosion shook the air. Plumes of flame burst high into the sky followed by black smoke.

Hayden studied the dark smoke as it curled upward "The fire caught the fuel lines of the helo."

Breathing heavily, Livy agreed. "Do you think they got away before the explosion?"

"I don't know. All I know is we have another fire to contend with. We need to climb down to the water. The best place to do that is at least another half a mile down the trail."

"Boyd and Dennis can climb. They'll be able to follow us."

"No, they won't. None of them carried climbing equipment. We'll clean ours up as we go down. Let's go."

He didn't mention that Boyd was one of the best free climbers in the world. He hoped Livy didn't remember that detail. She needed all the encouragement she could use. Right now, her positive attitude, the one he'd resented so much, was the most helpful tool in their survival arsenal.

They kept up their brisk pace until they reached the place with the climbable cliff. Hayden called a halt. "Let's rest here. Drink plenty of water and open one of those MREs."

She dipped her head with a weary shake. "I'm not hungry."

Sliding out of his pack, he let it drop to the ground. With his finger, he lifted her chin until her gaze met hers. "You'll need your strength for the climb. Eat."

She closed her eyes and her whole body sagged. Fear and tension had worn her ragged. He couldn't stand the sight.

Wrapping his arms around her, he pulled her close and held her tight. "Don't give up. Not yet."

She buried her face in his chest. "They almost killed us, Hayden…for a crime that's already been exposed. The FBI knows about their plans. Why do those men still need the files?"

He inhaled slowly and looked up at the sky, feeling as worn as she sounded. "I don't know, Liv. I guess they're scared of someone finding the proof to put them behind bars."

Clutching his shirt, she said, "I… I just need a minute."

Keeping her hands pressed against his chest, she stepped back. He liked the way those hands looked, close to his heart, so slender and yet so capable. He was almost sorry when she let them fall away. She walked to a nearby rock and plopped down.

He was weary, too. But he couldn't let his guard down. Not yet. They had too far to go. Grabbing one of the MRE containers and a bottle of water, he walked to the edge of the trail and looked down to plan their route.

The cliff was not a popular spot so it was rarely climbed. He couldn't see any hooks. He would be blazing a new trail. Thankfully he carried a small hammer. Livy had one, too, and she would need it to clean the hooks out as she came down. They couldn't leave anything for Boyd to use...if he survived the explosion. But they'd have to move quickly. The men were after them—and the helicopter fire was closing in.

He glanced back. The black smoke was still heavy but had spread wide. White as well as black smoke plumed upward. Black smoke meant materials—leather, plastic...the helicopter. White smoke meant natural elements, such as grass and brush. The fire had obviously spread to the surrounding meadow.

Tension spread through Hayden. They had to get moving. Rest was over.

Downing the last of the large water bottle he rose, stuffed the trash in his pack before hooking it over his shoulders. "I'm going down. Follow me when you're ready."

EIGHT

Livy watched Hayden replace his hiking shoes with his softer climbing ones. Then he stepped into his harness and unrolled his ropes. He stood on the edge of the cliff, looking calm, focused and determined. His lean form was silhouetted against the tall, dark granite cliffs. His beard shadowed his features, and he wore a slight frown of concentration. Livy tried to look away, but she couldn't. His confident form had become too dear to her.

When that man threatened to shoot Hayden, her blood had turned to ice. She couldn't speak, couldn't tell him everything he wanted to know fast enough. She would have stepped in front of that bullet before she would have let them shoot Hayden.

That was the moment she knew she loved him. Truly loved him. It wasn't a crush or infatuation. It was the real thing. She loved his sense of honor, how he'd taken care of everyone on this trip. Loved his confidence and composure that gave everyone courage, even her. She even loved his ever-present frown. She knew it for what it really was: concern for everyone around him.

Beneath Hayden's sometimes gruff exterior he cared,

really cared, not just about the hikers but about her. She felt safe in his hands, safe in his arms and she hadn't wanted to leave their warm protection when he held and comforted her. He didn't understand her faith, but that hadn't stopped her from falling for him.

When this was all over, she would have to find a way to go on without him. The thought made her heart twist, but no matter how much she loved him, she could not be with a man who didn't share her faith. She absolutely could not.

Placing her elbows on her knees, she covered her face with both hands.

Lord, help us get through. Help me *get through not just this but everything that will come after. I need You now in more ways than one.*

After a moment, she wiped her frustrated tears from her eyes, grabbed her backpack and hurried to the edge. He'd already hammered the first hook into the rocks, locked the carabiner onto it and started his descent. He worked steadily, hammering hooks into place, and climbing from finger- and toehold to the next.

When he reached a somewhat stable place, he called up to Livy. "Get started. Take your time. The first fifty feet or so are slippery. Don't rush and make a mistake."

Livy nodded and waited as he placed a hook to the side and moved his descent to a new position. Now, if she fell, he would not be below her and would have a better chance of stopping her. But Livy would not fall. She was determined to be as sure-footed and strong as Hayden.

She slid over the edge, belly first, and found a toehold. Sliding the tip of her shoe into the crevice, she found a fingerhold and lowered herself down. She was tired and weak. Her muscles felt like overstretched rubber bands.

This was going to be harder than she imagined. She was thankful Hayden had commanded her to eat. Surely, energy from the MRE would kick in eventually and help her power through.

She found her next toehold and eased down. Hooking her carabiner into the next round metal circle, she pulled her hammer off her pack and pulled the hook above her loose from the rocks. They might need these hooks again farther down the mountain…not to mention they couldn't leave anything behind for Boyd to use if he survived the helicopter explosion.

She moved cautiously as she kept climbing down and removing hooks. Hayden was right. The upper portion of the cliff was slick granite. She had scrapes on both hands and the pads of her fingers were getting raw. At long last, she reached the midway point. This rocky surface was as slick and loose as the top portion. It took all her strength and concentration to keep moving.

She paused long enough to rest. That's when she smelled the smoke. She'd been concentrating so hard, she hadn't seen the smoke curling over the edge of the cliff above her and rolling down.

She made a small sound.

"Don't let it spook you, Livy. Just think about your route and your next handhold. Don't look up."

The sound of his voice calmed her. She nodded and did as he told her. Searching for her next toehold, she moved down, got situated and removed the next hook. She worked like that for a long while until burning embers began to float down around her. At that, she couldn't help looking up.

The fire was a hundred feet above and to their left, advancing quickly toward the edge of the cliff directly above them.

A large branch had rolled to the edge of the cliff almost directly above where Livy was climbing.

"Stop cleaning, Livy. Just climb down!"

Once again, she did as Hayden bid her, searching for toeholds and fingerholds as she moved from one to the next. Embers flew in the air around her and the smoke was so thick it made her cough. Sweat poured into her eyes. Her hands were slick. One finger bled, making it harder to grip, and she still had a good fifty feet to go.

She felt a tug on the rope below her as Hayden jumped to the ground and landed in the only sandy spot of the riverbed. Once his feet were planted, he looked up.

"Release, Livy! Let me belay you down."

Something splashed in the water a short way up the river, but Livy didn't look to see what it was. She was too busy preparing to release. She dropped her rope down to Hayden. Taking a deep breath, she poised with her feet on the cliff wall before releasing.

"Livy, don't move." Hayden's voice was low and strained.

With the rope gripped tightly in both hands, she halted and looked down. Hayden had hold of the rope, but his gaze was fixed upriver.

Livy turned and looked over her shoulder. A large brown bear had tumbled down the mountainside and now lay sprawled on the edge of water. Upriver, other animals were climbing or jumping down to escape from the fire, running along the riverbank to safety. But the bear was closest. He seemed to be gathering his senses after his fall. He rose, shaking the water from his fur. His gaze fixed on Hayden, and he stood on his two hind legs.

The bear bellowed a furious growl. Falling to all fours, he barreled toward Hayden, racing down the edge of the river, splashing water and roaring all the way.

Livy gasped. "Hayden, climb back up here!"

"He's coming too fast. I'll never make it."

He was right. He wouldn't get ten feet up before the bear reached him and…bears could climb, too.

Livy's heart jumped to her throat. She couldn't speak or breathe. She was frozen in terror.

Above her something exploded. Another pine tree had caught fire. Debris flew over the edge. One branch as large as Livy's leg fell toward them.

"Hayden! Look out!"

She lunged to the side, away from the falling log, lost her footing and banged into the wall. She grunted in pain as her shoulder slammed against the granite, knocking the breath out of her. She clung to the rope. It jerked again as Hayden, still attached to her rope by his belay plate, jumped away from the falling log. Livy banged painfully into the wall again.

She clung to the rope as she spun in a circle. She watched the log crash down on the ground, right in the spot where Hayden had been standing. It shattered and fiery embers flew in the air. Some landed on Hayden. He cried out and quickly brushed the them away from his clothes.

Upriver, the charging bear froze. One look at the

fiery log on the ground and he spun, choosing the river over the fire. The current caught him and immediately swept him downriver, far away from Livy and Hayden.

She heaved in relief, but that emotion didn't last long. Looking down, she saw the log had landed on their rope where it was still coiled on the ground. Hayden was kicking at the burning log, trying to dislodge it, but he was losing his battle. Giving up, he jumped high and grabbed the dangling rope with both hands.

"Come on down, Livy, before it burns through."

Her shoulder still hurt but she gripped the rope and spun to get her feet against the wall. Bracing them, she pushed away. Hayden released the rope and she slid twenty feet down, bouncing against the cliff and pushing off so as not to hit the jagged edges of the rock. When she was close to the ground, Hayden tugged on her legs to pull her sideways, away from the fiery log beneath her feet.

When she finally touched down, Hayden grasped her in a bone-crunching hug that hurt her shoulder.

"Drop your harness and head down river! I'm going to see if I can get our rope loose from the hooks above. We might need it again."

Livy unhooked then hurried to the river's edge. Downriver was another canyon with steep walls and no walkway. The river current sped up through the narrow path. This terrain was as dangerous as the place where Ron had fallen in. One misstep and they'd both be swept away.

Unsure if she should go forward or wait for Hayden, she glanced back. He was still pulling the rope through the hooks in the cliff wall. She started back to help when the pine tree at the top fell sideways and rolled toward the edge.

"Hayden! It's coming down!"

He looked up just as the fiery tree dropped. He scurried away. The burning pine crashed to the ground amid flying embers. Scrambling backward, Hayden paused long enough to unhook the ignited rope from his belt. He tossed it on the ground and grabbed Livy. She threw her arms around his neck and her shoulder screamed, reminding her of her injury.

Trying to ignore the pain, she murmured, "I thought I'd lost you to that bear."

Hayden shook his head. "So did I."

He looked back at their rope on the ground. Most of it was smoldering or fully engulfed and a thin thread of flame traveled up it along the cliff.

"Come on. We need to get away from here."

He took her bad arm and Livy made a small sound.

"You're hurt." He stepped back to examine her.

"I banged my shoulder against the cliff wall. It's just a little sore. That's not our biggest problem."

She gestured to the river. "There's no more bank to walk on. We'll have to go into the water."

He studied the rocky wall above the water. "Look, there's a deep crevice about four feet above the water."

Then he frowned and studied her. "Do you think you can hang on to it?"

She looked up at the fire. Waves of smoke were rolling down into the canyon. In addition, more wild animals were trying to escape the fire and coming their way.

She shook her head. "I don't think I have a choice. We can't stay here."

Hayden nodded. "All right. Don't take a step until you're sure you have a good hold. Got it?"

She barely heard him over the noise of the fire above. She'd never thought about the sounds a fire made. Even on the day Mr. Miller had died, she'd been far enough away from the blaze that she hadn't really heard it. Now it was just above them. It roared louder than the bear and moved like a living creature, cracking branches and breaking its way through the forest.

"Did you hear me, Livy?"

She dragged her attention back to Hayden and nodded.

"I'll go first. I can catch you if you slip."

"I won't slip."

She meant every word. She wouldn't be a burden for Hayden. She absolutely refused to be.

She watched where he placed his fingers as he gingerly stepped into the water. For a moment, his foot slid off a moss-covered rock. But he didn't lose his balance. His fingertip grip on the crevice helped him stay upright. "Be careful."

She nodded again. Then she placed her fingers where he had placed his and stepped into the river. The icy water chilled her immediately, and she shivered. She wanted to jump back out, but she forced herself to focus on her footsteps. Thankfully, the water was clear, and they could see the rocks below. That made the trek a bit easier.

Just as they neared the bend in the river, there was a loud splash behind them. A large deer with massive antlers lunged into the river. The current caught him and swept him downriver, past them. He made it across to the opposite shore, but other animals did not fare as well. A family of raccoons waded into the water and quickly disappeared. Livy searched the rapids, looking for some sign of them but found nothing. She was forced to focus on her own progress.

Smoke filled the canyon, making breathing difficult. It was hard enough to move forward but then, a flurry of squirrels scurried along a ridge above them, scattering small rocks to rain down upon them. Hayden and Livy both stopped and ducked to shield their faces. Once the squirrels passed, they continued their movement through the icy water.

At last, they turned the corner of the bend. They were only a few feet away from dry land. Livy sighed with relief. But as soon as her feet touched dry ground, Hayden grabbed her hand.

"Come on. We're still not safe."

They hurried down the riverbank until the roar of the fire faded and no more animals scurried past them. The smoke had cleared, making the air easier to breathe. But Livy's feet were still frozen from the cold water, and they ached.

Too tired to go on, she dropped to the sandy ground. Hayden fell beside her. Ignoring him, she quickly removed her wet socks and climbing shoes. Pulling dry ones out of her pack, she eased them onto her feet and sighed. The socks may have been dirty from the previous day's use, but they were dry and warm.

"You're bleeding." Hayden reached for her hand.

With her feet aching from the cold, she'd forgotten about her scraped hands. The small finger of her left hand had been rubbed raw and was bleeding badly.

Hayden pulled tape from his pack. Taking her hand in his, he wrapped the finger.

Numb and exhausted, Livy watched his movements in a daze. His hands were warmer than hers and she couldn't help sighing with relief and easing into him.

He pulled her close with one arm around her. "Take a drink before we get going again. We need to put more distance between us and that fire, not to mention Boyd and his partners."

"You think they survived the helicopter explosion and the fire?"

"I don't know. There hasn't been any sign of them so far. But we're not taking any chances. We're moving as far away as possible.

He rubbed both her arms forcefully, careful not to jolt her shoulder. Then handed her an opened bottle of water.

She took it gratefully, drank her fill then tied the shoelaces of her hiking boots. She also tied her wet climbing shoes and socks onto her pack. They needed to dry before she used them again or put them back inside her pack. And they would surely need them again when they reached the stretch of river below the Mist Trail. The only way to reach the trail was to climb up the cliff walls.

Livy couldn't think about that right now. All she wanted was to get her feet warm.

Too soon Hayden stood and held his hand down to her. Gratefully, she gripped it and let him pull her up. "You did great back there. I can't think of anyone who could have handled that climb and the crawl through the water as well as you did."

He squeezed her hand then released it. Grabbing his pack from the ground, he led the way.

Did he mean it or was he just trying to encourage her? As he strode purposely from rock to rock and climbed through bushes without looking back, she felt certain he was just trying to encourage her. He must have been able to tell that she needed it. The thought of the climb out of the river gorge stayed at the back of her mind.

As the sun climbed high in the sky, Hayden never slowed or stopped. This stretch of their journey was as difficult as anything they'd encountered. He kept up a brutal pace. Several times Livy was tempted to simply drop to the ground and stop for good. Only the thought of disappointing Hayden kept her going.

They climbed along the bank, over logs, through branches hanging over the water and over boulders. It was exhausting work. Livy's mind drifted. She stumbled on a large boulder and almost slipped all the way down into the water. Thankfully, Hayden grabbed her pack and halted her slide. Frozen for a moment, they both just sat on the rock, taking deep breaths. At last, Livy crab-walked backward until Hayden wrapped his arms around her and held her. She leaned back against him, letting the sun-heated rock warm the fear-driven chill sweeping through her body.

Hayden held her tight and leaned into her. "You're right. It's time for a rest."

That made her laugh, and she relaxed against him, exhausted. "Next time I won't get your attention in such a drastic way. I'll ask first."

He laughed, too. They sat for a while and he never released her. She rested her cheek against his arm. A longing to stay there, sheltered in his arms, filled her. She was too tired to think of the future or to have regrets. She just enjoyed the moment. They were far enough from the fires that the air smelled sweet. The sky was clear and Livy was content.

At long last, he gripped both her arms and gave her a little shake. "Crawl over me and let's get off this rock. I need to filter us more water."

In their long trek down the riverbank, they'd used all the water the airman had given them. They climbed off the rock to a shallow sandy spot just beneath it. While Hayden filtered water to fill their drinking bottles, Livy used the cool river water to wash her hands and wipe down her face. She felt better afterward and drinking down half a filtered bottle restored her even more. Hayden refilled the bottles again, then extending a hand, pulled Livy to her feet one more time.

Refreshed, Livy felt more alert and aware. She noted that every twenty-five feet Hayden would look back behind them, scouring the area. Fewer animals attempted to cross the river as they fled the fire. But there were still some and they'd kept up a continuous racket behind them. For a long while now, it had been quiet. But Hayden seemed to watch the trail behind them as closely as ever. Had he spotted something…or someone behind them? Did he think those men were following them again?

She'd been so busy trying to keep up, she'd stopped looking behind. Now she was conscious again and she, too, began to search the area behind them. Occasionally, they'd hear another splash and look back to see an animal attempting to forge the river. But after a while, the path was too difficult. Livy stopped looking. She was so tired, it took all of her concentration just to keep her footing.

The sun dipped behind the mountain. Shadows made seeing their path even more challenging. The air grew cool. Livy was thankful they were working so hard. If not, she would surely have been cold. At last, they came around a bend and suddenly, Livy realized another reason Hayden had been pushing so hard. They were close to the Mist Trail. But here, the river narrowed again. This canyon was steeper and the current more treacherous. There was no way they could navigate the river using the cliff wall as they had before.

Livy looked up. They were going to have to climb. They had no ropes, and her shoulder had stiffened to the point of being almost useless.

She scoured the cliff, searching for a path, any way to climb. She found one but it would be difficult, maybe even treacherous. She held up her hands. Her fingers were scraped and raw. Her little finger was still bleeding through the wrap, and her shoulder was stiff. She wasn't going to be much help. Thankfully, Hayden had a reputation for being the best free climber in the world. Or at least, he had been. Granted, she hadn't seen him free-climb in a while. In fact, she'd never seen him free-climb.

Why hadn't...

She turned to him. His features had twisted into a mask of horror.

Panic shot through her. "What is it? What's wrong?"

He didn't answer but she had a terrible suspicion she knew what the problem was. But she wasn't ready to face that answer yet, so she didn't press. "It's a tough climb but we'll rest tonight and tackle it in the morning. We'll take it slow."

He shook his head. "I can't do it, Livy."

"Of course, you can. I… I'll slow you down. You'll make better time if you're not watching out for me. You can get help and come back for me."

"I can't do it."

"You're not listening. I won't drag you down. I'll wait for you here and—"

"Livy! I can't free-climb. I haven't been able to do it since the accident three years ago."

Stunned, she stared at him. He couldn't free-climb? But even as her mind repeated his words, memories fell into place of all the times she'd seen him climb. He never climbed without ropes. Not once in the year she'd known him. She thought of his extreme focus on safety and his intensity when he did climb. It wasn't just his personality to be cautious. He was concentrating, trying to overcome his fear.

It suddenly all made sense. She should have seen it. Should have known. But once again, she'd made her most fatal mistake. She'd placed her faith and all her trust in a human being, expected them to fill the holes in her life, to do more, to be more.

Disappointment and despair swept over her as she realized neither one of them could move forward. They were trapped. Her legs gave out, and she slumped to the ground.

The pain on Livy's face horrified Hayden. Wisps of her blond hair had come loose from her ponytail long ago and feathered into her face. Dark circles smudged below her eyes. She was exhausted, and this disappointment seemed to undo her.

He dropped to the ground beside her. "I'm sorry, Livy. I should have told you."

Silent tears fell down her cheeks, devastating Hayden. He hadn't felt this useless, this helpless since the day Tommy died. "I'm sorry, Livy, so sorry. I should have told you I'm a broken man. I'm a failure."

He tried to reach for her, but his hands trembled and he let them drop to his lap.

She looked up and wiped weakly at the tears on her cheeks. "You're not unique, Hayden. We're all wounded. And I'm not crying because of your failure. You didn't fail. You got us all out of the fire. Eight people, including me, are alive because of you. You stood up to the men who were aiming a gun at us, put your life before mine. I'm not crying because of you. I'm crying because *I* failed."

Surprise shook him. "What are you talking about?"

She wiped her cheeks again, but tears continued to fall. "It's the same mistake I make over and over, Hayden, the one I tried to explain to you the day I apologized. My mother was mentally unstable. Her doctors said she had the worst case of bipolar disorder they'd ever seen. One minute she'd be the best mom—loving, fun, caring—and then something would happen. It would be like a switch flipped and she'd turn into a monster. The change was so rapid and so extreme, we'd be having great fun one minute and the next minute she'd be screaming violently and slapping me. I was constantly confused and terrified. I remember crying and praying for the good mommy to come back. Finally, my dad took her to a hospital for help. I'd only see her when she was well, so I started to believe my prayers had been answered. When I graduated, she told me how proud she was that I'd overcome the hereditary illness we shared. I felt on top of the world, like nothing could stop me. But the medication never fully worked for my mother, leaving her to struggle through her symptoms on her own. The battle wore her down. Not long after my graduation, she killed herself."

Waves of hurt washed over Hayden. He understood that kind of pain, had felt it himself the day Tommy fell.

He'd wondered so many times about her past, now he knew the depth of it. Her pain matched his. Just like him, she'd fought a dark war.

He shook his head. "It wasn't your fault, Livy. I'm sure you and your dad did all you could to help her."

"Yes, we did. But it wasn't enough and what's more, my dreams hadn't come true. You see, I thought my well-being depended on my mom's good health. If she could conquer her depression and be successful, so could I. When she failed, I didn't know how I could possibly succeed. I put my faith in a human not God."

"I don't understand. Of course, you would have hoped and wanted your mother to be healthy."

"No, you don't understand. I believed my health, my sanity depended on my mother being healthy. I placed my hope in her getting better and leading the way. But she was a human. When she failed, I was sure I would fail, too."

"Your mother couldn't stop what happened to her. It wasn't her fault."

"That's true. We fail but God never does. He doesn't make mistakes, and He wants the best for us. He made it so that when our strength runs out, we can draw on His. All we have to do is lean into Him. When I realized my ability to heal came from Him and not my mother or my own frail will, then I started to get better. I learned how to make my relationship with Him strong and drew courage and power from Him. That's how I learned to deal with my illness and face the world. He's never failed me, Hayden. It's only when I expect things from people that only God can do that I run into problems."

"So what are you saying?"

"That day when I apologized, I was trying to explain to you what I had done wrong. I was beginning to feel like you could do anything. I was expecting too much out of you when I should have remembered you are only human."

He shook his head and looked away. "It's wrong to have expectations of people."

She touched his chin with her fingers and gently turned him back to her. "No, it's not wrong to expect things like trust. Honor. Kindness. Responsibility. I can expect those things from you and never be disappointed because you have them in abundance. What you don't have is the faith to carry you up that cliff."

"Faith wouldn't carry me up that wall and it certainly won't carry you."

"No, you don't have that kind of faith. But I do and it will."

He leaned away from her. What she was suggesting was ridiculous. Just wrong.

Livy took a deep breath. "I need to eat and rest. I'll be ready in the morning."

There was that foolish positivity again. The certainty that she could conquer mountains.

"That's absurd. It's too difficult. You'll fall."

She smiled, the sweetest most loving smile he'd ever seen. "Then I'll die knowing I'm in the Lord's hands, Hayden. I'll be doing what He wants me to do."

He wanted to scoff, to call her a fool. At the same time, he yearned for the comfort that showed on her features. To have that kind of faith was a gift. Knowing that someone stronger, kinder, gentler was guiding his path and that he'd be safe in His hands would be a blessing.

As a climber, Hayden chose the path. He found the way. It was his choices that led to the tragic fall that took his friend away. Only he was responsible.

He shook his head. "What I wouldn't give to know that someone else was to blame for Tommy's death."

Livy froze. "You want to blame God for the accident?"

Hayden sent her an angry look. He couldn't help himself. "If He's an all-knowing, all-powerful God, why did He let it happen? Why did He let Tommy die? I should have been the one to fall."

At his words, Livy's expression softened. It was a look so kind, so loving it almost undid him. He longed to pull her into his arms, to absorb some of her light and peace and...love. He wished for all the world he could draw it into him and store it up as a counter to the darkness inside him.

"Hayden, I'm so sorry that happened to you. I don't know why it did, but I do know God has already forgiven you for whatever mistakes you might have made. And I know He hears your heartfelt wishes. Maybe if you just ask, He could help you learn to forgive yourself."

"Perhaps I *can* forgive myself but how will that help us now? It's fear that keeps me from climbing, not guilt."

Some of the glow surrounding her faded.

She shrugged and turned away. "Maybe. I don't have all the answers. I just know who does."

Wearily, she climbed to her feet. "I'm cold."

She walked to the sun-warmed cliff wall and leaned her back against it. Sighing, she eased down, pulled out her MRE package and opened it.

Frustrated, Hayden walked to the edge of the river to filter water. He filled one bottle for her. She took it from him with a simple thanks and went back to eating.

She was seriously contemplating a deadly climb with an injured shoulder, and still, she was filled with peace. It was the kind of optimism he'd resented since he first met her.

But now…he ached to have that same peace, to know God was in charge.

Was it really as simple as just asking for it?

Of course not. Nothing in life was that simple.

He returned to the river and looked up at his nemesis, the rocky cliff. He studied its sheer shape, angles and corners. He found toe and footholds, but they were too far apart for Livy's shorter reach. She'd never make it.

Anger filled him. He shook his head and whispered, "If You exist, don't let this happen. Protect her. She's worth two of me."

Silence was his response. No answers came. No sense of peace like the one that glowed from Livy.

What did he expect? Lightning bolts?

Disgusted, he grabbed his own MRE package. But as he ate, his glance strayed back to the wall. The more he studied it, the more he saw a path. It stood out as plain as day, almost easy enough for Livy's reach.

The light faded. The sun dipped behind the cliffs on both sides of the river, and still, he studied the wall in the dusky gloom. If he could find a good path for Livy...

He imagined himself moving from grip to grip, ledge to ledge. He visualized the way, climbing steadily all the way to the top. Then he started again from the very bottom. He pictured the entire climb for a second time.

Then he paused in shock. Usually, he faltered when he tried to mentally stake out a path. He couldn't even visualize a free climb without shaking and falling. It was the nightmare that haunted his dreams.

But this time, he hadn't hesitated. Not even once.

In his mind, he'd found a path and climbed it. Even now, the way stood out to him as if it had been highlighted. Visualizing the climb again, he almost felt his muscles moving and contracting. He knew which reach would stretch his arms to the limit. Which toehold would be precarious. He was able to picture climbing the wall without slowing.

If he could do it in his imagination, could he do it for real? Stunned, he visually imagined it again. As he reached the top, he paused in amazement.

For the first time in three years, he'd just routed a free climb without hesitation.

Was Livy right? Just ask and you shall receive? Was it possible? He had to know.

Livy was leaning against the rock, her head tilted forward, dozing. He didn't want to wake her, but he had to know, had to find the truth.

He hurried across the way and knelt in front of her. "Livy, wake up."

She jerked awake instantly. "What's wrong? What happened?"

He grasped her hands. "Livy, I just charted a path up the cliff."

Still lethargic, she nodded. "Okay..."

"Don't you see? I haven't been able to do that since the fall. It's the nightmare I have every night, falling when I try to climb without ropes. I haven't been able to even think of completing a free climb without falling. But I just found a way up, picturing the whole climb not once but three times and never faltered. I asked God to protect you, Livy, and then it happened. Is what you said true? All you have to do is ask?"

She gripped his hands and the most beautiful smile he'd ever seen lit her face. "Yes...yes that's how it happens. At least that's how I've survived."

"But would He do it for someone like me, someone who doesn't even believe?"

Her features softened into that kind, loving expression that had undone him before.

"He loves us all, Hayden. If for no other reason, He loves you because He knows how much I do."

The love pouring out of her warmed him, filled him to the brim with happiness. For the first time, he felt the peaceful glow that was so much a part of Livy. It surged through his being all the way to his fingertips and toes. He was so thankful for the feeling, he cupped her cheeks, pulled her close and kissed her.

She tasted like sweet water and peppermint chocolate, the tiny candy packed in their MREs. Her lips were cool and warm at the same time and so…very wonderful. Hope bubbled up inside him. Hope for a life free of fear, maybe even a future with this glowing, faithful woman.

He broke off the kiss, leaned his forehead against hers and said, "Pray with me. Help me ask Him for strength."

She nodded. Gripping his hands, she prayed. He took in every word, every new praise, like a starving man. Her words were liquid to a thirsty soul.

Peace filled him and soon, he joined her in prayer, repeating words that were new to him and praising a God he'd never truly believed existed.

At long last, Livy grew tired and leaned into him. He held her in his arms, basking in the light she'd shared with him. It filled him up, warmed him as Livy drifted to sleep.

He believed.

Wonder filled him. Tomorrow he would climb, and they would live.

They would live!

Then just as he was about to fall asleep, he heard a sound. A rustling and a splash. It echoed down the smooth flowing water. It could have been a log falling in the river or another large animal…maybe even one of the men that still might be behind them.

Normally, his over cautious self would have been

filled with concern at the thought that Boyd and his partners could still be alive. He probably would have spent the night worrying. But tonight, the belief that someone greater and more powerful than himself was watching over them gave him peace. No matter what happened, they were in God's hands. He would lead the way. Hayden felt comforted and full of hope...especially when no other sounds followed the splash.

Smiling, he leaned his head against the cliff wall. In the morning, he would climb the cliff and get them to safety. He closed his eyes and prayed for the strength he needed.

NINE

Livy woke before Hayden. He'd slept peacefully all night but she'd been restless. After the first few hours of rest in his arms, she couldn't seem to get her shoulder in a comfortable position. It ached and the pain wore her down. She was close to giving in to it.

Then she'd remember Hayden's amazing change. She'd never dreamed he might believe—and especially not so quickly and with such conviction. As carefully as possible, she straightened to study his sleeping features.

His dark beard shadowed his lean cheeks and jaw. Two days and it had grown in fully, making him look more rakish than ever. But Livy knew the truth. He was a wounded man, one recovering from a hurt so deep, he hadn't seen any way out of the pain.

For the first time since they saw the firestorm whirling into a fiery tornado, his features were free from a frown. He'd found peace at last. For that she was thankful. She suspected the kiss, the affection he had showered on her last night was born of thankfulness, too, not love. He'd been so happy and full of peace, it had burst out of him in a show of affection. But she wasn't going to place her trust in what happened. He cared, truly cared for her. But love, real love, was about more. It was about total trust and companionship.

She and Hayden had that when they were climbing. They worked together, moved together. They even thought alike, often reaching for the same hold. It was like dancing together…but on the side of a cliff. That added an element of excitement that dancing never could.

She smiled.

But nothing could compete with the peace she now saw on his face. That was a true gift…a gift of grace and it gave her pleasure to think that she had played a small part in helping him find it.

No matter what happened in the future, she had a place in Hayden's life, a piece of him no one else would ever have. She'd be content with that.

She leaned her head back against the wall and closed her eyes, allowing Hayden a few more minutes of sleep. The sun peeked over the cliff across the river and its warming rays flowed over them.

Hayden stirred. Climbing to her feet, Livy took the water bottles to the edge of the water and filtered more into Hayden's bottle. She had one granola bar left in her pack. She retrieved it and sat back down beside him.

Reaching over, he pulled her hand off her lap, linked their fingers together and sat in silence. At last, he sighed and moved to rise.

She handed him the granola bar. "You'll need the energy for the climb."

He silently took the bar and split it. "You'll need your strength, too."

She smiled, determined to show a brave face, and popped it into her mouth. He drank heavily from the bottle she'd filled. Then he walked to the edge of the river to splash water on his face. Shaking the loose drops from his hands, he turned to study the cliff face. She watched him as he mentally charted a path up the sheer wall.

When he finished, he looked at her. "Pray with me?"

She rose to her feet, gripped his hands in hers and spoke the words she needed to hear as much as he did.

When she was done, he kissed her forehead. "Thank you...for everything."

Then, without another word, he stalked to the wall, dipped his fingers in his pouch of chalk and began to climb. At first it was easy. He scaled the steep walls without hesitation, moving gracefully and quickly. But soon he slowed, not because he was tiring but because the wall was so difficult. He'd said he'd found a path but search as hard as she could, Livy couldn't spot a toehold or foothold for him to grasp. Stalled, he stayed poised for a long while. His legs began to tremble and then his arms.

He was losing his hold on his confidence. His hope was slipping.

Livy prayed out loud, calling out the words of her favorite psalm. "Though I walk through the valley of the shadow of death..."

Her words seemed to give him confidence. He reached across an impossible chasm and slid his fingers into a crevice so tiny, Livy could not see it from the ground. With sheer strength, he pulled himself over and found a small notch of rock to balance his foot on.

Then in another breath, he skimmed over to another, safer handhold, and leaned against the cliff to rest.

Livy released her breath. Just then, she heard a splash. She spun and saw Boyd Goldberg coming around the rocky point. He was staggering so badly, he could barely put one foot in front of the other. His clothes were torn. His face was black with soot and his hands were so badly burned they oozed. She could only stare as he stumbled toward her.

"I knew if I was patient, I'd get you."

His voice was raspy and weak, but his gaze was intense...almost rabid. He looked half-mad with pain and yet, he never slowed. He marched toward her, wavering from side to side.

"It's all your fault. Why didn't you just let Miller die? We had it all planned...everything right down to the minute and then you showed up. You had to save the day, didn't you? You and him. You had to be so perfect and so righteous. Now I've lost everything...my career, my wife, even my cousin. Everything. But you're going to pay. Both of you."

He kept coming toward her, she backed up against the wall. As soon as she felt the rock against her back, she dodged away, not wanting to be pinned there. She edged toward the water and Boyd followed her.

"Leave her alone, Boyd!" Hayden shouted from the wall.

Livy glanced up quickly, not daring to look away from the man advancing toward her for too long. Hayden was climbing back down as fast as he could, but would he reach her before Boyd could strike?

No. She needed to defend herself. She dared to take

her eyes off Boyd and looked around for something to use as a weapon. She glanced down. She was on the edge of the river. Through the glimmering water she spied round, palm-sized river rocks. She remembered how Hayden had thrown the rock at Dennis.

"It's me you want, Boyd. I'm the one that caused you problems, not Livy."

Hayden's shout pulled Boyd's attention off Livy. She bent slowly and cautiously, never taking her gaze off the man so close to her.

Boyd looked up and nodded. "Yes, and for that you're going to suffer. You'll lose one more person you care about. Even if you survive, you'll live with the fact that you weren't able to stop the death of one more loved one." He nodded again as if notching a mark in his mind.

If Livy had any doubts about his sanity, that little movement sealed it. Boyd wasn't rational and Hayden would never get down in time. She would have to stop him.

She quickly stooped the rest of the way down and grabbed rocks in both hands.

Boyd saw her and growled like a wild animal, lunging forward. Livy pulled back her arm and threw one rock with all her strength. It went wide and splashed in the river. Boyd snarled and moved forward but Livy let loose with the other stone. This one hit him squarely in the center of his chest just below his Adam's apple. He choked, grabbed his throat and stumbled back. He lost his footing on the mossy rocks. Arms flailing, he yelled as he plunged into the water.

His head bobbed up quickly and his arms plowed

the water, reaching for the shore. But the current was too strong. It had him firmly in its grip and it swept him downstream before Livy could even step out of the water. She'd already stooped to pick up another rock. Now she dropped it, instinctively moving toward him.

"Don't, Livy! Stay out of the water!"

Hayden yelled at her from twenty feet above. Releasing his grip, he dropped to the sandy beach beside her and rolled to break his fall.

In seconds, he was up and lunged toward her. "Come on!"

They only had fifty feet of shore before the cliffs jutted into the water again, blocking their path. Around the rocky bend, the river straightened into the stretch that Ron had fallen into. It was only a football field's length from the falls' drop-off. The current there picked up as if it were racing toward its fantastic dive off the side of the mountain.

If they were going to stop Boyd from going over the falls, they'd have to reach him before he went around the bend.

Hayden raced down the beach. Livy followed, but not nearly as fast. Hayden was in place long before her, eyes glued to Boyd, who was coming close to the shore and the rocky point.

Hayden grabbed a long branch off the riverbank. Stripping off his shirt, he dropped it to the ground then pointed to a tree with branches hanging over the water.

"Place your feet against that tree trunk. Brace yourself and hold on to me. Don't let go or I'll get caught in the current, too."

She froze and stared at him.

He gripped her hands. "You can do this, Livy. Plant your feet and pray for all three of us."

She shook her head, not certain she was strong enough to hold Hayden against the current.

"Help me!" Boyd's panicked shout shocked her into action.

She climbed over the rock to a point behind the tree. Its trunk bent over the rock, its branches reached for the water. The pitch of the rock was steep and it was all Livy could do to keep from sliding into the water. At last, she had her feet braced and she nodded to Hayden.

He climbed over her, lay down on the rock and slid, belly first into the river. He caught his breath in a gasp as his bare chest encountered the cold water. Livy gripped his feet and clung to them.

Hayden drifted downstream. The branch in his grasp banged against him, threatening to break him loose from Livy's grip and drag him downstream, too.

A thousand thoughts chased through Livy's mind as she clung to Hayden's jerking feet. Did they have a chance of saving Boyd? Why was Hayden risking his life for a man who hated him—a man who wanted him dead?

Because it was who Hayden was. The man who scaled mountains and risked his life to rescue others. He couldn't let Boyd die without trying to help and neither could she.

Those thoughts flashed through her mind as Hayden fought the branch and the current. She struggled to hang on to his booted feet, and silently prayed.

The current pulled on Hayden, tugging on his body with enough force to almost dislodge Livy. Clearing her mind of all thoughts except for her prayers, she focused on maintaining her hold on Hayden's boots.

Hayden struggled to keep his head above the water as he shoved the branch out in front of him. Amazingly, the current was sweeping Boyd toward them. He was coming at a fast pace. If Hayden could extend the branch just a few feet more…

With a mighty effort, he pushed the sodden branch out of the water. It flew high in the air and plopped down on top with a splash that caught Boyd's attention. With weak strokes, he swam toward the extended branch and finally managed to grab the end of it.

He had hold of it with both hands!

The current dragged Boyd farther downstream. He clung to the wood, but his injured hands slid down the branch, catching on the multiple stubs of smaller offshoots. He cried out in pain.

"Hold on, Boyd! Hold on! I'll pull you in."

With superhuman strength, Hayden pulled the branch closer to himself. His years of climbing gave him the power to tug on the branch, but Boyd continued to slide downward. He whimpered, struggling to hang on with his badly burned hands. He was only a few feet away from Hayden when he looked up. He met Hayden's gaze. Some semblances of sanity returned, and he shook his head.

Hayden shook his head, too. "No…no…don't. I won't let you…"

Boyd let go. Simply let go.

Hayden shouted in protest. Livy cried out as Boyd drifted away, sweeping around the bend and out of sight.

Shocked, silent tears slid down Livy's cheeks. Weak

with disappointment, Hayden bobbed in the current that still tried to pull him from Livy's grasp.

"I'm pulling you out!" She slid his right foot up and hooked it around her waist. Then she did the same with his left. She tugged and pulled on his legs until a good portion of Hayden's body was on the rock. Using his arms, he propelled himself the rest of the way, sat up and turned to face Livy.

She threw herself into his arms and he held her. He was shivering from the freezing water. They sat on the warm rock for a long while, holding each other, shaking with shock and distress.

Suddenly, a cry echoed back to them, swept up by the air currents.

Boyd had gone over the falls.

Livy buried her face in Hayden's neck. He held her close, and she let the tears fall.

"Do you think he gave up or did he choose to die rather than let you be the one to save him?"

"If I know Boyd, he chose to die. You heard him. He lost everything—his wife, his cousin even his career. All he had left was his vengeance. He must have understood that Tommy's death almost destroyed me. He wanted to hurt you to get at me, but that failed. When I tried to rescue him, I think it might have given him one last hope…that guilt over my failure to save him would consume me. He sacrificed his life for his vengeance."

She leaned back to search his face. "But you won't let it consume you, right?"

He nodded and pushed a strand of hair behind her ear. "Guilt might have destroyed me a few days ago. A man without hope is lost. But now I have hope."

He smiled. "Someone told me I was forgiven, and I believed it."

Touched by his words, Livy tucked her head in the curve of his neck again. They sat for a long while, letting the sun warm them and drive away some of the shock.

But sooner rather than later, Hayden stood and pulled her up with him. He climbed off the rock, pulled his shirt back on and stretched his weary back and arms. His gaze drifted to the cliff, and cold swept through Livy again.

The threat from Boyd was gone. But they still were not safe. Garanetti was still unaccounted for—and there were fires closing in all around them. Hayden had to climb the cliff in his exhausted, weakened state to get help.

Livy's heart sank. Even a forgiven man had limits to his strength.

For the second time in the space of a few days, despair poured into Livy. It was so strong, it brought her to her knees.

Hayden stooped beside her. "What's wrong? Are you all right?"

She couldn't speak the words, couldn't tell him that she'd lost all hope when he'd just found it. She couldn't fail him when he needed it the most.

Faking a smile, she gave a brief shake of her head. "I guess my legs are a little weak after holding on to you. You're heavier than you look."

She reached for him, and he helped her get to her feet. They walked back down the beach where they'd left their packs.

She eased down in the crevice where they'd slept. The rocks warmed her. It was just what she needed.

Hayden refilled their water bottles and brought one to her. Then he eased back against the rock and closed his eyes to rest. After a long while, he stopped shivering. Maybe he even dozed off. But Livy stayed awake praying for the strength and courage to send him on his way.

After a long while, he murmured, "I don't want to leave you alone down here."

Gathering all her faith, she managed a shaky smile. "I'm never alone. My best friend is always with me."

Laughter broke out of him and he shook his head. "I should have expected that."

Her faith and laughter seemed to give him what he needed. He rose to his feet. Livy stood also, a bit renewed, and determined to believe her own words.

She handed him his water bottle. He hooked it on his belt. His chalk bag was soaked so Livy gave him hers. He belted that on as well. With one last kiss to her forehead, he shifted his shoulders and studied the cliff face. With hardly any hesitation, he moved forward, and reached for his first handhold.

Hayden climbed steadily. He was weak. His arms and legs strained with each grip and step. But he didn't stop. He couldn't. Livy was counting on him. This time her positivity didn't fool him. He recognized it for what it was. Conviction. Faith in the face of the impossible. She chose to believe in God's love for her even when everything told her to give up, to give in because they were doomed.

She *chose* to *believe*.

And now, so did he. God would be with him no matter what. Sweat pooled on his back and face, pouring into his eyes. He paused to wipe the stinging drops away and chalk up his fingertips again. He was reaching the forty-foot mark…the place where he had faltered before.

Don't let me fail, Lord. Not for my sake but hers. She's endured so much. Help me bring her out of this.

He reached the spot where he had to stretch across the space. His legs and arms were so fatigued, he wasn't sure he could make it. He made the mistake of looking down. Dizziness swept over him. Panic filled him. He grabbed for a crevice with his right hand. The precipice was weak and gave way. Rocks cascaded down the cliff and his hold slipped. His foot slid off and he dangled on the cliff with one arm.

Waves of panic swept over him. His arm and fingers burned. He dared not let go long enough to reach into his chalk pouch.

Livy's voice drifted up to him. "Though I walk through the valley of death, I shall fear no evil…"

He took a deep breath and joined her prayer. "…for thou art with me."

The words echoed through his being, pressing down on the rising panic. He dipped his fingers in the chalk then looked to his right. The hold he wanted was within reach. He swung his leg over, found a small toehold and pressed up. With the pressure off his left arm, he could reach farther with his right. Gripping a small ledge with his fingertips, he pulled himself across the space to a place of safety.

Below, Livy whooped and cried out, "Thank You, Lord!"

Smiling, Hayden whispered. "Yes, thank You."

He rested a moment longer. Then gathering himself, he searched out his path again. It was right before him, the same track he'd gone over three times in his mind last night. He could see it as clearly as if it were highlighted with markers.

Filled with confidence, he grasped the next hold and the next, climbing with renewed confidence. He didn't pause or look down again but continued to repeat the words of the psalm and focus on them.

Suddenly, he realized he was reaching for air. He'd climbed to the top!

Smiling, he crab-walked sideways to the hold he'd spied from below and pulled himself onto the top of the cliff. Rolling to his back, he stared up at the blue sky and laughed out loud.

He rested for a long while…until he heard Livy calling his name. Then he rolled over and got to his feet. His legs almost gave out beneath him, they were so tired. But he was there at the top, he'd almost reached the end. He wouldn't give up now.

He couldn't see Livy below, so he stumbled to another spot on the cliff top and peered down. "I'm here, Livy. I made it!"

She moved out away from the cliff wall and waved. "I knew you could do it!"

He waved again, anxious now to get help, to feel her in his arms and to rest with her there.

He was only a few yards from the trail. He stumbled toward it. His legs were still shaky, but he had to move. He couldn't leave Livy down there any longer. He found the trail. It descended. He recognized where he was—

just a few hundred feet from the falls trail. They'd come a lot farther than he'd thought. Hopefully, he'd make it down the steep trail without falling.

He walked and walked until his feet didn't seem to want to work. They dragged when they should have lifted. He slid downward and almost fell. Bending over, he grasped his knees to rest. If he sat down, he might not get up again. Inhaling, he slowed his breathing and quieted. In the distance, he heard voices. He froze, listening intently.

Yes, it really was voices.

"Hey!" The word came out raspy and weak. He swallowed and licked chapped, dry lips, then tried again.

"Help! I'm here!" His tone was stronger now. He stumbled toward the sounds he'd heard but they'd stopped. Had he imagined the voices?

He couldn't hear them anymore, but he kept moving downhill, slipping and sliding as he went. At last, he turned the corner of the trail.

Firefighters in bright yellow vests with shovels in their hands were running up the path toward him.

Releasing his breath in an exhausted sigh, Hayden let himself drop to the ground.

TEN

Hours had passed since Hayden leaned out and waved to her. Alone and too tired to think anymore, she leaned against the rock wall and watched the dusky shadow's edge creep toward her. They'd lost precious light trying to save Boyd.

She shook her head. She wouldn't allow that thought to discourage her. She didn't regret trying to save the man, no matter how undeserving he was, and she knew Hayden didn't regret it either. Of all the things she loved about Hayden—his amazing strength and competence as a climber, his brooding good looks, even his persistent frown—the thing she loved most was his integrity. His determination to do right no matter what.

Even if he didn't know it, he had always been a man of faith, a man marching to the inner tone of God's voice. Now that he had actually heard that voice, and received God's mercy, Hayden was a complete package. A man she could love with all her being. If Hayden's feelings for her had changed as well, maybe there was hope for them. But first she had to survive.

She was getting weaker by the moment. It took all

her effort to cock her head and look at the shadows creeping closer. Soon they would reach her. Without Hayden's body heat, it would be difficult to keep warm. If she fell asleep, she'd freeze. It was that simple. Stay awake or die.

Shaking her head, she rose from her warm spot and went to the river's edge to filter more water. A cold drink of water would help her shake off the lethargy seeping through her.

Sitting at the river's edge reminded her of a gospel song. She sang it out loud, sipping the water to refresh her dry mouth. She sang louder and louder but soon was so tired, and cold, she stumbled back to the wall. Snuggling into the last sunny spot, she closed her eyes. But just for a minute.

She dozed off and jerked awake, heart pounding.

"Lord! Keep my eyes open and my heart turned to You."

She took another sip of water. But her eyes drifted shut again. This time, the sound of something splashing through the water nudged her awake.

"Oh no, not again." Half-asleep, she murmured the words out loud.

Then her eyes flew open, and she stared at a three-foot fawn standing on the edge of the river, not more than ten feet away. He was soaking wet. His spindly legs trembled as he shivered from the cold.

Livy looked all around, up and down the river for its mother. But there was no sign of another deer. The pair must have tried to cross and gotten separated.

"Are you alone, little one?"

The tiny animal's ears flicked back and forth, but

aside from that tiny movement, it stayed frozen in a wary stance.

Trying not to spook it, she continued in a low tone. "I'm all alone, too. I won't hurt you, I promise."

She didn't have any food to share, and she dared not move for fear the frightened creature would bound away and end up in the water again. So, she closed her eyes, leaned back and dozed. Better to sleep now so she could stay awake after dark.

When she woke next, the little fawn had curled up next to her and was sound asleep. His little warm body was a comfort.

She smiled. "Good. We both need the body heat."

The sun was nearly gone, the shadows creeping close to her. She needed to stay awake now. The rock would stay warm for a long time but soon, the cold would take over the deep crevices in the canyon and she would freeze if she slept.

She thought of Hayden—his smile, his tender touch, his kisses, the one of passion and the other, gentle touch to her forehead, like she was precious. Very precious.

Her eyes dipped closed. In her mind, Hayden smiled at her, pushed a straggling strand of hair behind her ear. He whispered her name. She loved the sound of her name on his lips. He said it so softly, so low and loving. She could spend the rest of her life listening to him say her name.

But now he was yelling. His smile turned a frown as he spoke louder. Something rained down on her. Hayden was yelling and dropping things on her.

Livy jerked awake as rocks trickled down on top of her head. Despite all her efforts, she'd fallen asleep.

Then she heard her name again. It really was Hayden! He was calling her. More rocks tumbled down. She looked up. Two members of the search and rescue team were rappelling down the cliff!

Hayden made it! She was rescued!

She climbed to her feet and stumbled back to see the top of the cliff. The little fawn jumped up and leaned against her. She could feel his little body trembling. Bending, she scooped him into her arms and looked up.

Hayden was once again leaning over the edge of the cliff, searching for her. She called out and a brilliant smile burst out of the dark shadows of his beard.

"Be patient, Livy! They'll reach you in a few!"

She nodded and clutched the fawn. She knew the two men from Hayden's search and rescue team. The first to reach her was Joe Russell. He unhooked from his belt.

"Boy, are we glad to see you!"

Livy laughed. "Not half as glad as I am to see you! Do you have something to eat?"

"That's the same thing Hayden asked." He handed her a small, opened package of trail mix. "We have more up top."

She nodded. "Maybe this'll give me the strength I need to climb."

"You won't be climbing. We'll hoist you all the way up. Put the deer down."

She shook her head. "No, the fawn goes with me."

"Livy, it'll be hard for you to get up with it in your arms."

She shook her head. "It'll die if I leave it here. It has to go with me. I can't leave it alone."

Joe seemed to recognize the desperation in her tone. He nodded.

"All right. We'll figure it out."

He unhooked another harness from around his waist and handed it to her. She wrapped one arm around the fawn then pulled the harness up.

"You'll have to buckle it."

Joe stepped forward, and the fawn reared back, its little legs kicking. Joe froze.

Livy soothed the fawn, speaking to it in low tones until it calmed. By that time, the other team member, Ray, had arrived. He slowly reached for the fawn.

"Give it to me, Livy. I'll make sure it gets up top safe."

"No, it'll be calmer with me. Just help me get hooked up."

Joe cinched the belt and attached her to the rope while she poured handfuls of the trail mix into her mouth. She handed the half-finished bag to Joe.

"Can you give it a little? It's as hungry as I am."

Frowning, Joe poured the rest into his open palm. The fawn sniffed the nuts, then lapped them up in one gulp.

Joe met Livy's gaze and smiled. "Come on. Let's get you two up top."

They hoisted her up the cliff wall. All she had to do was make sure she stayed clear of the rocky points. She pushed away from the cliff with her feet while murmuring comforting words to the animal.

At the top, Hayden and the firefighters pulled her up on the ledge.

Hayden reached for her as if for a hug, but the animal was in his way.

"I see you found a new friend."

She nodded. "It was alone, too."

Her tone sounded tearful even to her own ears.

Hayden grasped her arms. "We'll take care of it, Livy."

She smiled but tears seeped out of her eyes and trickled down her cheeks.

Reaching over, Hayden wiped the tears away. "When you didn't answer me, I was afraid a wild animal got to you."

She laughed. "A wild animal *did* capture me."

The surrounding men of the crew laughed, too. Hayden put one arm around her. "Come on. We still have a long walk ahead of us."

Forty-eight hours later, Livy parked her car in front of the park's museum patio and hurried around to the other side to help Maggie out. They'd both spent the last two days in the hospital. They were dehydrated. Livy's shoulder was badly bruised and had to be wrapped securely against her body. Maggie had a broken bone in her ankle. They'd finished her cast this morning and released them both. Jenna and Raul had picked them up from the Fresno Hospital.

It delighted Livy to meet her new goddaughter, Rachelle Olivia Holguin. Livy sat in the back seat next to the infant seat and talked to her goddaughter during the entire hour drive home. Little Livy was the spitting image of Jenna, and Big Livy couldn't take her gaze off her pert little nose and black curly hair. She imagined if Hayden ever had children, their hair would look just like Little Livy's.

Raul and Jenna dropped them off at the hotel. Maggie and Livy stowed their gear in their suite then took Livy's car to the press briefing. Dale and the other officials had waited for them to return before holding this event since they were both receiving commendations. The other members of Maggie's team, Pruitt and Gault, had already been called to another crime scene in the Northwest.

Livy pulled Maggie's crutches out of the back seat and handed them to her. Her friend was sore and moving slowly. Livy tried to get her to skip the award ceremony and stay at the lodge, but she was determined to attend.

She slid out of Livy's Jeep and cringed as her foot hit the pavement.

Livy shook her head. "I tried to tell you...."

Maggie shook her head. "I've waited two days to get some closure on this. I'm not waiting another hour."

"Suit yourself. But don't blame me if you're too sore to move for the rest of the day."

She shut the car door as her friend placed the crutches in front of her and swung into motion.

Livy was just as eager to find some resolution...and to see Hayden. She hadn't heard from him since she'd stepped into the ambulance headed to the hospital. He'd only spent a few hours in the park's clinic for dehydration and then had been working with the ISB team and Dale, writing reports and debriefing.

A lot had been resolved while she and Maggie were in the hospital. They had heard a few details. One of Livy's friends had taken over the care of the little fawn.

She sent it to a rescue facility that helped wild animals move back into the wild. Livy wished she'd had a chance to say goodbye to her wilderness friend, but the ranger reminded her that the less human contact the little fawn had, the better its chances of moving back into the wild.

The forward progress of the complex fire had been momentarily halted. The firestorm winds had died down, allowing firefighter planes to fly and drop retardant. Apparently, their efforts had an impact. They had hopes of keeping the complex fire contained and even driving it back on the burned-out areas to put it out completely.

They had put the two fires along the trail out. That information had been released to the public. But Maggie and Livy had heard no other details. Nothing about Garanetti, Dennis and Boyd, or if the FBI had been able to uncover any of Miller's files.

As they walked toward the building, Livy quailed. Tension tightened inside her. Hayden had not tried to reach out to her since they'd parted ways. That pretty much answered any lingering doubts she had in her mind. They had shared a catastrophic event. What they had been through together had given them a special bond. They were good working partners and friends. But that was as far as Hayden's feelings went.

His tender kisses and words had meaning, but not the kind Livy yearned for in her heart.

She was prepared for their meeting today, had gone through it in her mind many times. Now she just had to make sure she saw it through and didn't break down or say something that would hurt their friendship.

She helped Maggie over the curb and across the

crowded patio. Many reporters and officials were attending this ceremony. In fact, it was so crowded Maggie and Livy could barely get through. She could just see the top of Hayden's head in one corner. Reporters surrounded him, holding microphones in his face.

Ranger Armstead saw them and hurried across the space to hug Livy. Then he gave Maggie a one-armed hug, too. He introduced them both to the National Park Service's lead ranger for the western sector, Henry Ortega.

"Let me just say how relieved I am to see you two in one piece," Ortega said.

Armstead agreed. "It's amazing to me you all made it out alive."

Maggie nodded her head in Hayden's direction. "We wouldn't have if not for Hayden and Livy. They were fantastic."

Ranger Ortega nodded. "We're aware. That's why we've planned something special for them."

Livy frowned. "Special? What kind of special? I'm looking forward to things getting back to normal."

Dale smiled. "Let's just say you might be able to visit Maggie in DC."

Maggie smiled. "Awesome! We'll get our spa day after all."

Livy laughed and shrugged. "I guess so."

Ranger Armstead motioned to the podium. "Why don't we go up on the dais? We'll have a little more privacy there. We have a lot to share."

Once Livy and Maggie were seated, Rangers Armstead and Ortega turned their backs to the crowd, facing the seated women.

Armstead spoke in a low tone. "We have so much to tell you, I'm not even sure where to start. I'm assuming you know about the fires."

Livy nodded. "I still can't believe Dennis was willing to start them and let everyone on that hike die just to get to Hayden and me."

Armstead nodded in agreement. "You weren't the only ones. Apparently, they were after Ron, too."

She sighed. "He claimed that was true. He was terrified when the fire on the trail started."

"He had a right to be. Garanetti was determined to fix the situation, to kill everyone involved, including Ron. Dennis knew enough about fires to keep the first one moving toward the water, so it was controlled. But by the time he started the second one, the complex fire had created its own wind currents that blew the second fire back on them and they were trapped, too. During your flight down the river, firefighters put out both fires. We were afraid we'd find your bodies in the aftermath. Instead, we found three bodies in the meadow— and the burned wreckage of the helicopter."

"Three?"

"The helicopter pilot lost his life as well."

Livy looked at Ranger Armstead. "What about Boyd?"

His steadfast gaze filled her with relief. "His body was found downstream."

She closed her eyes at the mental image of his body, shattered from the fall over the cliff. Some victims of the falls were never found. But Boyd had been recovered and now he and his partners in crime were all dead.

She and everyone else were truly safe. Their evil

rampage had been stopped, but the incident wasn't completely over.

She shook her head. "All the witnesses are gone. Lyra Enterprises, the one who started this with their plans for Hetch Hetchy, are getting away scot-free."

Her boss smiled. "They're not getting away. A visitor reported seeing Miller hiking along the valley loop near El Capitan. We took search dogs out there and found a bear pack hidden beneath some rocks. Inside were all of Miller's files. There was enough information to keep the FBI and Interpol busy for months."

Ranger Ortega nodded. "Of course, Lyra is claiming they knew nothing about Garanetti's or Boyd's illegal actions. They played their denials fast and heavy. In fact, they were even bold enough to ask if Hayden would become their representative."

Armstead agreed. "That was before we found the files. Now we have proof of their illegal activities, including bribes paid to Blankenship. We have all we need to shut them down."

Maggie grinned and raised her hand toward Livy for a high five.

After they hit palms, Livy frowned. "Wait! That's it! That's what Miller was trying to tell me. Remember? He gave me the El Capitan charm for my bracelet. The day he died, I thought he was just chattering from shock, but he was trying to say 'charm'! He wanted me to know he'd hidden the pack on the trail by El Capitan."

She closed her eyes, frustrated that she'd missed the clue. "I could have avoided so much danger and the deaths of four people if I'd just realized sooner."

Armstead patted her shoulder. "Don't blame your-self, Livy. Men like Boyd always seem to be one step ahead of the good guys. If I'd listened to Hayden when he first called my attention to Boyd's actions, all of this could have been avoided."

She looked over his shoulder into the crowd. Report-ers still surrounded Hayden. In fact, he looked as if he was trying to escape.

"There's more," Armstead added, his features som-ber. "When Boyd disappeared a few days ago, Paulette came to me. She asked for protection. Apparently, years ago, Boyd confessed he sabotaged Hayden's equipment the day his partner fell. Boyd even showed Paulette how he did it. She wanted to go to the authorities, but he threatened to kill her if she ever told anyone. She's spent the last two years suffering under his abuse and fearing for her life."

Shock swept over Livy at Boyd's cruelty…then a dif-ferent cold seeped through her. Hayden was innocent. His reputation was restored. Now that he'd conquered his fear of free climbing, he could return to his former life. That's why Lyra had offered to hire him.

He could even resume his engagement with Paulette.

A weight settled in Livy's stomach. Of course, he would want to return to his old life. Why wouldn't he want the world's recognition, now that his guilt was no longer standing in his way? Who wouldn't want that kind of chance to regain all that he had lost?

Cold seeped through her body one inch at a time. How could she not want that for him?

She couldn't. She had to let him go. Not only was there no hope for a relationship between them, but

Hayden would also probably leave the park forever soon. Tears burned her eyes, and she had to look away.

About that time, Hayden finally broke free from the reporters and hopped up on the podium stage. He headed straight over to Livy, hugged her and kissed her forehead.

"I'm glad you stayed an extra day at the hospital. You look much healthier."

She smiled and nodded. Then he went straight to Maggie and gave her a hug. "It's good to see you looking better. I understand the ankle is broken."

Maggie gave a shrug. "Yeah, only *I* could successfully break my ankle on a five-foot drop."

Hayden hugged her again, looked about to say more, but the reporters called his name and shouted more questions.

Ranger Armstead said, "I guess I better get this show started or we won't have any peace."

He stepped up to the podium and adjusted the microphone. First, he introduced Ranger Ortega, who officiated the ceremony. The lead ranger outlined the dangers they'd faced, the steps they'd taken. Then he broke down each contributor's actions. He gave Maggie a commendation for her perseverance after her injury. Then Livy, for her courage and determination. Hayden was the last. Ranger Ortega described how he had led the two of them to safety and climbed their way to a rescue. Then Ortega outlined how the parks department was hoping to put Hayden's skills to use at a specially designed crisis management school for all employees of the national parks.

Ranger Ortega hesitated. "As I'm sure you all know,

Hayden has many other opportunities coming his way."
He turned slightly to face Hayden behind him.

"But I'd like to let him know how much the parks department wants him to stay with us. This is just a small token of how we hope to proceed."

He handed Hayden what looked to Livy like a check.

"This is our first investment in the school we'd like you to run."

Hayden took the check and shook Ortega's hand. He nodded his thanks and stepped up to the podium to say a few words, but before he could, reporters started shouting questions.

"Will you be accepting the park's offer?"

"That depends," Hayden replied. "It's too soon for me to be making any long-term decisions."

"Is it true you've been asked to be the spokesperson for three major climbing equipment manufacturers?"

Hayden nodded. "Yes, it's true."

"Will you be taking over Lyra's school in Hetch Hetchy?"

Hayden heaved a sigh. "A consortium has offered to buy the resort. Since there were so many illegal activities at the facility, the authorities have asked me to look over the equipment and training program to make certain it's safe so the sale can proceed."

"You've agreed to do it, right?"

Hayden paused and looked at Livy. His expression seemed as if he was seeking understanding. "There are one hundred employees already on staff with their jobs on the line. So yes, I've agreed to examine everything so that the sale can proceed and those people can keep their jobs."

"When will you start?"

"I'm leaving for Hetch Hetchy in an hour. As I said, many jobs are depending on things going smoothly in the takeover."

Livy's heart plummeted. One hour. They wouldn't even have time to say goodbye.

She was prepared to let him go, but she'd hoped for… what? To prolong the pain? To watch and want more?

No. better for him to leave now. To let him move on with his life so she could move on with hers.

Ranger Armstead thanked the folks attending and ended the conference. People swarmed Hayden once again. Rising slowly, Livy handed Maggie her crutches, led her off the podium and went straight to the car.

Livy didn't dare look back at Hayden. She knew if she did, the burning in her eyes would turn to real tears. She kept her gaze in front of her…on the future.

ELEVEN

On a crisp, cool November afternoon, Livy nodded to Ranger Armstead's secretary.

"Go on in, Livy. He's waiting for you."

Livy smiled and opened the door. She'd been gone from the park almost a month. Maggie, being the good friend she was, knew Livy was hiding her devastation at Hayden's abrupt departure so she asked Livy to help her fly back to her home in Washington, DC.

Livy had laughed and said she didn't think she'd be much help since her shoulder had not yet recovered.

"Well, since I only have one foot, together we'll be able to make a whole. Come on. It'll be fun."

Thankful for the offer, Livy took the extra leave time the park department offered her. When they reached Washington, Maggie took Livy to her favorite restaurants. They toured the sights and the parks' national headquarters. Just before Livy's flight home, they had their spa day. Of course, Maggie couldn't get the full works with her foot in the cast, but she sported some bright orange toenails.

After leaving Washington, DC., Livy flew to Los

Angeles to visit her dad. It was good to see him, to talk
and share. She said little about Hayden, but her father
knew her well. She suspected he read between the lines
and knew she'd fallen in love.

She hadn't heard from Hayden in almost two weeks.
During her first week in Washington, he'd texted her
several times. The messages were bland, with simple
questions about her health and how she was doing. She
felt like they were pity texts, maybe to apologize. She'd
stopped answering him the second week of her trip and
they hadn't spoken since.

After her week in Los Angles was up, her dad had
followed her back to Yosemite. He'd said it was to visit
Jenna and see her new baby. But Livy knew him well
enough to understand that he was worried about her. But
he didn't need to worry. Livy really was determined to
move forward no matter how much it hurt.

Now that she was back at the park, moving forward
meant lots of peaceful, long hikes. Today, she decided it
was time to revisit the Mist Trail, so this morning she'd
waved goodbye to her dad and headed out.

As she left, he said, "Don't be gone too long. I'm fix-
ing my homemade spaghetti, and I invited Jenna, Raul
and Little Livy over."

Livy had smiled. Dad was determined to keep her
busy. "I'll be back in a couple of hours."

She was scheduled to return to work in two days, so
she paid this quick visit to her boss to check in before
her hike. She opened the door. He was on the phone.

He motioned her in while shaking his head. "No,
Hayden Bryant isn't in the park, and before you ask, no,
I don't know how to reach him. Goodbye."

He hung up the phone and shook his head again. "I get at least four of those calls a day."

Livy shrugged. "He's in big demand."

Armstead gestured to the chair in front of him. "You're not exactly lost in the commotion. I've gotten quite a few calls about you, too. In fact, I had one this morning from a magazine asking for an interview."

She shook her head. "I'm not really interested in talking about what happened. I'm ready to move on."

He heaved a sigh. "I suspected as much."

Fiddling with something on his desk, he paused. "You know, Livy, you can take more time if you need it."

"I'm fine, really. It will be good to get back to work."

Still, he fiddled with the paper clip. "I can understand that, but I also think it might be…tough to be back here. You know, Ranger Ortega has assured me you could have almost any position you'd like. Of course, I want you back, but if it's too hard… I'll push a transfer through for you."

Livy paused. As much as she loved this park, it might be better to take another position. There was only one thing she would miss.

"I need to be able to climb."

He nodded. "We can find a place with that for you, Livy. I'll make it work if it would help."

She met his gaze. Concern was written on his features. Did he know her true feelings about Hayden? Was she that obvious?

Probably. She was an open book. Sighing, she nodded. "I'll give it some thought. Thanks."

Waving goodbye, she headed out the door and drove straight to the Mist Trail trailhead. It was a cloudy day and snow was in the air. But she needed to think, to get above everything in her head so she could have a clear perspective. That meant hiking and a good spot to look down on the world.

She hadn't been on the trail since that fateful day when she hiked it with the group. It was time to face the memories and put them where they belonged…in the past.

She set a strong pace. The pine-scented air felt clean and cold. Soon she was breathing hard, pumping out the past with each heavy exhalation. By the time she reached her first lookout point, she was panting, but she felt refreshed and energized.

Shadows had fallen over the valley and lights twinkled on. The valley and the buildings looked like a miniature Christmas village. Just then, tiny snowflakes began to fall.

Livy closed her eyes, turned her face up to the flakes and let them kiss her cheeks. This was what she needed. She felt closest to God and gained her strength here. She wasn't ready to leave the park. Not yet. There were other beautiful places. Spots where she could spend time with the Lord and have new adventures. But right now, she needed to be here.

She heard a noise behind her and turned.

Hayden walked toward her. She gasped. "What are you doing here?"

He smiled and his teeth flashed white against his

dark beard. "Looking for you. I stopped by your house and your father said I would find you up here."

"You met my dad?"

"Yeah, he invited me to dinner and sent me after you."

Livy heaved a sigh. That sounded like her dad. Surely, he knew how difficult dinner with Hayden would be?

She looked back on the valley's tiny, Christmassy lights. If Hayden was going to be in the park, staying here might not be an option.

She cleared her throat. "Did you finish the job at Hetch Hetchy?"

"Yes, everybody went back to work yesterday."

He came to stand beside her and looked out over the valley but didn't speak. She glanced at him sideways once…twice.

When he still didn't talk, she said, "Paulette is a free woman now."

"Yeah. She's free from Boyd's abuse. She suffered so much under him. But I'm sure she has a hard road back to true mental freedom. You would understand that better than anyone. Maybe you could talk to her, share with her what you taught me about faith."

He wanted her to minister to the woman who would take him away from her? Livy was so stunned, it was a long moment before she could gather her thoughts.

"Sure… I'll help, but you can talk to her, too."

He frowned and nodded slowly. "I will. I want to thank her for coming forth with the truth. It means a lot to me."

He grew silent again, just stared at the valley below.

Livy was confused and uncomfortable. "What are you doing here, Hayden?"

"I suppose the same thing you are. Enjoying the view."

"No, I mean…why did you come back? You…you can have your old life back. You can be an international star again and travel the world."

"Yes, I suppose that's true. But right now, I'd like to head back down the trail so we can eat your dad's spaghetti. It smelled amazing."

She huffed. "Hayden, you can have everything you lost. You can—"

He shook his head and pulled her around to face him. "Of course, I can. With you and Jesus by my side, I can have everything!"

"Oh…" Livy's exclamation came out in a breathless whisper. Did he mean…

Laughing again, Hayden bent down and kissed her. His full beard tickled her cheeks. Warmth spread from her lips to her toes. She felt weak and tingly, and so wonderful…but it had happened too fast. She needed to step back.

She pushed him at arm's length.

"Wait…you can't just waltz back into my life after leaving me hanging for a month and make assumptions like that. I have needs and plans, too. Why didn't you tell me how you felt?"

He pulled her back into his arms. "Everything happened so fast, we were both spinning. If it was up to me, I would have run off with you right there and then, but I wanted to give you time to sort through your feelings, to be sure of what you wanted."

She inhaled deeply. She couldn't argue with that… much. But she was going to try. "You could have told me that."

"Yes, I could have, but I was confused, too. And I didn't want to pressure you. The day of the conference, you looked shell-shocked and overwhelmed. I'm used to reporters and crowds like that, but I knew it was all new to you. I needed to step back and think about what I might be asking you to do if I went back to that life. But after a few weeks without you, I had my answer. I'm ready to leave all that behind if it means I can be with you."

"Oh." The word came out in a breathless gasp again.

But Hayden didn't pause. "That's why you're up here, isn't it? To sort through your thoughts and decide what you want?"

She nodded, silently, not quite ready to forgive him for a month of pain, even if he did it for a good reason.

"But," he went on, "what I should have said is with Jesus by *our* side, *we* can do anything. I can't decide where to go until you say yes."

Her lips parted in surprise at his sudden proposal. Unwilling to bend just yet, she shook her head. "You have to ask me first."

He wrapped his arms tighter around her waist and pulled her closer, so close his lips were inches away. Then he spoke in low tones. "Olivia Chatham, will you join me in the next greatest adventure of my life? Will you be my wife?"

He had said the right words at last. With all her concerns swept away, Livy brushed the snowflakes off his dark beard, cupped his cheeks with both hands and kissed him.

"I would love to be your partner on that journey, Hayden...wherever it takes us," she said when she finally broke the kiss.

He smiled. "With Jesus by our side, we can do anything."

Then he kissed her again.

* * * * *

Dear Reader,

For the past four years, I've been fortunate enough to live just forty minutes away from Yosemite National Park. We've spent many day trips exploring the park, including some of its quieter paths and roads. That's when I learned that every October climbers flock to the park for climbing events. At the end of the month, the climbers organize into groups to clean up after Yosemite's busy summer visitors. Just one of the hidden details you're able to discover if you are a full-time RVer like we are.

My son was a firefighter for Cal Fire Wildland fires for ten years. He shared his many adventures with me. One of the first things he told me about was the noise a fire makes. Of course, he'd been taught that fires were loud, but even he was shocked during his first big fire by the explosions, roars and winds that a wildland fire can create. Those winds can lead to complex firestorms that generate fire tornados.

Two years ago, we were asked to evacuate because of the complex Creek Fire. We stayed at the local fairgrounds and watched as, day after day, people evacuated their horses and cattle away from the fire. Even after we were given the go-ahead to return, the air was thick with smoke and stayed that way for two weeks. It was quite an experience.

Naturally, all those pieces of information had to come together in a story. I hope you enjoyed *Yosemite*

Firestorm! If you are interested in reading more of our motor home adventures, you can follow my newsletter at https://www.subscribepage.com/c7i1q9.

Blessings!
Tanya Stowe

COMING NEXT MONTH FROM
Love Inspired Suspense

SCENT OF TRUTH
Pacific Northwest K-9 Unit • by Valerie Hansen

National park ranger Brooke Stevens knows she's innocent of homicide, yet all evidence points to her. Officer Colt Matthews and his K-9 partner must investigate when a dead body is found in Brooke's backyard, but seeking the truth could prove deadly.

CRIME SCENE WITNESS
Amish Country Justice • by Dana R. Lynn

Targeted by a serial killer, single mother Lissa Paige is attacked while cleaning a crime scene. Now US marshal Micah Bender is determined to protect Lissa and her child, deciding to hide them in Amish country. Can they uncover the criminal mastermind's identity before Lissa becomes another victim?

COLD CASE CHASE
by Maggie K. Black

FBI agent Anthony Jones never expected the most challenging fugitive he'd ever have to track down would be his childhood sweetheart, Tessa Watson. Framed for a crime she didn't commit, can Tessa trust Anthony to help her clear her name before the real killer silences her forever?

TEXAS RANCH TARGET
Cowboy Protectors • by Virginia Vaughan

When a client is murdered under his watch, security expert Brett Harmon searches for answers to how the assailant got past his security measures. Amnesiac cybersecurity expert Jaycee Richmond just might have the information he's looking for...if he can keep her safe from a killer long enough for her to remember.

TUNNEL CREEK AMBUSH
by Kerry Johnson

After she's brutally attacked in Sumter National Forest, wildlife biologist Kinsley Miller must work with police officer and single dad Jasper Holt, her estranged ex-boyfriend, to figure out why she has a target on her back...before they both end up dead.

ALASKAN WILDERNESS MURDER
by Kathleen Tailer

Nearly drowning on day one of a new expedition, kayaking tour guide Zoey Kirk assumes it's an accident. But Josiah Quinn trusts his military instincts and is sure they're not safe. With the body count rising, Zoey and Josiah must work together to unmask the culprit before they strike again.

HARLEQUIN
PLUS

Try the best multimedia subscription service for romance readers like you!

Read, Watch and Play.

Experience the easiest way to get the romance content you crave.

Start your **FREE TRIAL** at
<u>www.harlequinplus.com/freetrial</u>.